LOOK ME IN THE EYE

Sílvia Soler was born in Figueres in 1961 and she is a writer and a journalist. She is the co-author of *Ramblejar* (1992), a journey through the history of Les Rambles, Barcelona's most famous street, and she has also written the short stories volume *Arriben els ocells de nit* (1985) and the novels *El centre exacte de la nit* (1992), *El son dels volcans* (Columna, 1999) and *L'arbre de Judes* (Columna, 2001). In 2003 *Mira'm als ulls* won the Fiter i Rosell Award. Her last titles published in Columna are *Petons de diumenge* (Prudenci Bertrana Award 2008) and *Una família fora de sèrie* (2010). She has also written the successful series of books *39+1*, *39+1+1* and *Per molts anys*.

Richard Thomson moved to Catalonia in 1986, where he learned Catalan from friends and FC Barcelona television commentaries. His translation of Jordi Coca's *Under the Dust* was published in 2007, and Coca's play *Black Beach* in 2008. Other works published include the play *Match Day* by David Plana (Teatre Lliure) and short stories by Francesc Serés and Pere Guixà (Dalkey Archive Press). He has also acted as Catalan–English workshop leader at the British Centre for Literary Translation, University of East Anglia.

LOOK ME IN THE EYE

SÍLVIA SOLER

Translated by Richard Thomson

Parthian
The Old Surgery
Napier Street
Cardigan
SA43 1ED

www.parthianbooks.com

First published in Spanish as *Mira'm als ulls*
© Sílvia Soler 2003
All Rights Reserved

This edition first published in English by Parthian 2010
Translation © Richard Thomson 2010

The translation of this work was supported by
a grant from the Institut Ramon Llull.

ISBN 978-1-905762-16-3

Cover photo © Steve Murez / Getty images
Cover design by www.theundercard.co.uk
Typesetting by Lucy Llewellyn
Printed and bound by Gomer

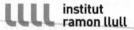

institut
ramon llull

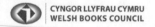

CYNGOR LLYFRAU CYMRU
WELSH BOOKS COUNCIL

Published with the financial support of the Welsh Books Council.

For Sílvia Mateu, who offers constant
and generous friendship, with a sense
of humour and a lot of patience.

Part I

Chapter One

I open my eyes. My head is still on the pillow. I try and find the energy, in some hidden corner, to get up. My thoughts are overrun by a buzz of little voices. What should I do? Acknowledge the pain, look it in the eye and learn to live with it? Or the very opposite: run away from thoughts of martyrdom and force myself to ignore the pain? Which option is braver, which more resigned? How do you run away from bitterness without falling into idiocy?

Is it right to accept freely the possibilities of running away? Does frivolity as a narcotic bring peace... or lead into emptiness? Is it good to swallow analgesics to forget the pain, without thinking? Should you let yourself be carried by inertia, floating comfortably down the river of the day-to-day?

I close my eyes again, unsettled by the drone of all this buzzing. I find a fresh piece of pillow to rest my cheek.

I think I have a fever.

Is it a kind of betrayal not to think about our dear departed? Is our remembering them every day, bearing and suffering their loss, a form of masochism? If a friend deceives us, should we pretend the wound isn't deep and will soon heal?

You have to be positive, be optimistic. That's the message I hear every blessed day. Well-intentioned friends, women's magazines, cancer patient associations, psychologists. Must I accept that the intelligent, healthy reaction is not to think about death, betrayal, sadness, pain, loneliness, all the things which cause us anguish and heartache?

I've always seen myself as an intelligent healthy person. Psychologically strong. Maybe it's not very modest, but that's the way it is. I'm brave when looking pain in the eye, but it's making me feel ill. I'm tired and sad. I feel alone. Perhaps it's time now to look elsewhere. Give in finally, and let myself be washed along by this water, sometimes calm, sometimes turbulent.

I shall let the river rock me into sleep as I listen to the murmuring water.

Blanca goes to the window. The morning is transparent, taut. The February sun, which should be subdued, dazzles her as she looks out at the tangle of aerials and the flowering almond tree on the neighbours' patio. She has a headache. She must have overdone the bourbon last night. But she has to get down to work. The publisher is in a hurry to get this Italian novel translated. As always, the first thing she did with it was peek at the last page. She can't help it. The last few words give her the tone of a novel.

She drops the book on the desk. It has landed spread wide open like the legs of a girl of easy virtue. Reading the little epilogue, she wasn't able to work out the plot, but the words have found their way inside her, breaking through the layers of her headache. She savours them again as she takes a sip of coffee.

... into sleep as I listen to the murmuring water.

She switches on the computer. The screen blinks. Blanca decides to take an aspirin with her coffee. She opens a new document and goes back to the first page of the novel. *Scordare il dolore. Forget the Pain.* She starts.

> *So... that's what love was like. Such a journey, so many hopes, to end up submerged in this sea of lies. I try to control the heat rising from my neck to my cheeks and the syncopated, frenetic dance of my heart inside my chest.*
> *'Bruna?'*
> *Massimo calls me from the shadows of the bedroom. He's been on call at the hospital all night and has just got into bed. I go to him to give him a kiss, approaching the bed in the dark. As he hugs me, I'm afraid he can feel my heart pounding like a drum.*

'Syncopated, frenetic'? Or perhaps it would fit better to say: 'wild, furious'. She looks in the dictionary of synonyms. 'Frenetic': irate, crazy, delirious, furious, excited, mad. She likes the image of a heart beating frenetically, but 'furious' is closer to the word in the original Italian, 'furente'.

The first words are always the most difficult for her to translate. As she makes her way through the text like someone walking a mountain trail, it seems the sentences start coming together more easily, as if her legs take on new strength, or the path flattens out.

Finally she chooses 'frenetic'. She likes it more. She reads the paragraph aloud. When she says '... the syncopated, frenetic dance of my heart inside my chest...' she smiles, satisfied.

She leans against the backrest of the ergonomically designed chair. She settles herself, planting her backside squarely on the seat, remembering the advice of the physiotherapist who deals with the seizures in her back. She stretches out her hands over the keyboard, making her fingers click. She starts to translate the second paragraph.

I go back to the hallway and put my hand into his coat pocket. I find Massimo's wallet and go through it with a desperation that any careless observer might confuse with enthusiasm.

'Desperation' and 'enthusiasm'. Two apparently contradictory terms which certainly can come together at the same time in the more visible aspects of a behaviour. Blanca imagines the novel's protagonist: the shortened breath, the trembling hands, a film of sweat on her forehead.... She picks up the book and looks at it carefully: *Scordare il dolore*. Title in red letters on a white background. The author's name, a shade darker, blood red, and in a smaller font: Matteo Spadaro. She'd never heard of him before. Sol had told her it was a debut novel. But apparently it's been a runaway success in Italy. Seven hundred thousand copies. Translated into six languages so far. And now into Catalan. *Forget the Pain.*

Blanca smiles: this Spadaro probably doesn't even know the language exists. 'Catalano?', he'll say with a quizzical look when his publisher tells him it's being translated. 'Barcelona', the publisher will say. And probably go on with 'Gaudí, Barça'. Or more likely, 'Barça, Gaudí'. How sad. Blanca sighs and looks for a picture of the Italian author on the cover, but there isn't one. Born in Naples. Lives in Palermo. This is his first novel.

What must life be like in Sicily? She'd love to go there. She'd probably love living there. As far back as she can remember, Blanca has wanted to live on an island, but without ever knowing quite why. She's always been convinced, obviously on no scientific basis, that people who are born on an island are special. Their space is more defined. Their world is a nugget of land with a natural border. She has always found it difficult to know where she is from. Her roots are spread around and her connections scattered. Friendships from here and there, before and now. She is sensitive to landscapes, can easily come to love them, but there is none she feels her own. She finds it difficult to explain. Even Raimon doesn't completely understand, nor her mother. 'You're weird,' she tells her fondly. They love her, but they don't understand her. For her it's exactly the opposite with her world. She understands it, but doesn't love it.

The telephone rescues her from all the broodings that go nowhere. It's her sister.

'Have you started the translation?'

Sol works for a publisher and commissions the translations. It's still hard to explain this kind of luck. Being able to work without any timetable or bosses keeping their eye on you. Battling with dictionaries, stopping when she wants and imagining herself in Sicily.

'Who is Matteo Spadaro?'

'I don't know much at all. A Sicilian who started writing in his thirties and seems to have the knack of connecting with his readers. I haven't read the novel though. What do you make of it?'

'I've only just started. But I like it.... What was it you wanted?'

'Just to say good morning.... Okay, just for you to say good morning to me. I've only been up for an hour and a half and I've already had a row with the pair of them. I don't want to start work in a bad mood.

Sol has two teenage sons, Raül who's nineteen, and Cèlia, who's seventeen. They're not especially difficult, but they can wind her up. Blanca knows her sister is tough and generous, precisely the two qualities you need when you're the mother of teenagers. But even so they exhaust her patience.

'What's happened?' asks Blanca, inviting her to unburden herself.

But Sol doesn't surrender:

'Nothing. The same as always. It's so boring I'm sick of it myself.'

'Tell me.'

'No. It's boring, and even more for you, you're light years away from all this...'

Sol is right. The six-year age gap between the sisters is insignificant in some ways, but here there is a chasm of difference. Sol got married very young and at thirty-six has a whole family past behind her. Blanca, at thirty, is still very young. She has no responsibilities and the world revolves easily around her and Raimon. What's more, her sister lost her husband very early on. She has been on a journey which has taken her further, infinitely further, than the six years that separate them.

Sol won't waste her time thinking it would've been nice to be born on an island.

'Have you ever been to Sicily?' Blanca asks now, in a not very subtle attempt to change the subject.

'Yes, years ago, with Jaume.'

Blanca bites her lip. She's screwed up. Instead of changing the subject she's buried her sister in gloom.

'We had a really great time! That's really set up my morning! Just thinking about that trip has really changed the way I feel!'

Blanca smiles. How come she doesn't know her after so many years? She realises that, as always, she needs to take notes with her sister. Sol is a masterclass in how to get through life. She gives her a mental hug and goes back to Spadaro's novel.

After a while I give up. I put the wallet back in the coat pocket. What was I looking for? I don't know. Some sign of betrayal. Gradually my heart recovers its normal rhythm. I'm left drenched in sweat. Under the hot water of the shower – it almost scalds – I try again to think I am wrong. I search for a convincing argument. I want my head to show my heart it is mistaken but my heart is very stubborn. It's a battle I've fought for months. A bloody battle that is destroying me. When did my life turn into this shit?

I think of the Bruna of a year ago, free of the suffocation, living without suspicion, and I am not able to remember how I was, how I felt. What can it have been like waiting calmly for him to come home, knowing he'd been at work at the hospital, greeting him with a trusting hug? I can't recall those days when I listened without disbelief as he recounted his day. Just interested, not analysing the words like a detective searching for traces of lies...

Traces or tracks? Traces sounds much better, doesn't it?

... traces of lies. Now I don't live my own day. I live his. Right now he must be having breakfast with her, now maybe they've got away from the hospital, now they're having lunch together, now he's taking her home.

I used to have an interesting life, I tell myself again as I wash my hair more roughly than necessary. I used to throw myself into my work; teaching was fulfilling, and I got on extremely well with my colleagues. I loved spending time with my daughters, and with friends.

I scrub my hair even harder, even quicker, the shampoo threatening my eyes. When was it I stopped enjoying going to work? When did I start to drift away from my friends? When exactly did I cease to be myself? As I try to work it out I am pulling hard on my hair, hard enough to hurt.

I need to see a psychiatrist, I think to myself for the umpteenth time. I think about it every day, two or three times. And I will in the end, but not with any confidence. The problem isn't within me. Or is it? Does the problem really exist? What if I'm ruining my life for no sound reason? That would mean Massimo was right: I'd have turned into a neurotic who'll end up destroying our marriage.

I get dressed quickly. I can hear the girls squabbling

in their room next door. If I don't get a move on all three of us will be late. I gently open the bedroom door a chink. I can hear Massimo's measured breathing, seemingly calm. He's fallen asleep already. He must be so tired. I feel guilty about thinking horrible things of him. Isn't he the man I love? I can't envisage him doing anything bad to me...

'Flavia, Giulia! Come on, we're going to be late!'

They look at me all sleepily. They're still little. They still don't know anything. They still feel protected at home and at school. They don't know their world could crumble in an instant. I take them by the hand and leave the house, forcing myself to rinse away negative thoughts, the same as I'd done with the shampoo which had been about to get in my eyes.

'Hello, is that the Dictionary Shop?'

Hearing Raimon's voice was like a cuddle. She liked the tone, halfway between affectionate and sarcastic, that he often adopted to get her going over her obsession with dictionaries. 'They'll be evicting us from the house soon,' he'd say.

'How's it going?'

'Oh fine, nothing much. We're on a break and I was thinking about you. I wanted to say hello.'

'Hello.'

'Hello.'

Blanca feels a warming between her thighs. Raimon's last hello has undressed her. He darkened his voice and enounced the two syllables slowly. She knows for sure he's thinking about last night, although she doesn't say so.

'What time does the rehearsal finish?' she asks, almost giggling.

'At two. Can I come back for lunch?'

'I've got nothing ready... but yes.'

'As long as you're ready that's plenty.'

She says a soft goodbye and hangs up, a smile on her lips. Life really is much more pleasant when there's love. She thinks about Sol. Thinks about her mother. Thinks about Bruna. She feels fortunate, almost privileged. What must it be like to be widowed? What must it be like to be betrayed? Hmm. She doesn't want to think about it. Neither of the two. Both things seem equally impossible. But they're not, obviously. She reckons it's best not to think about it.

She remembers what her friend Anna had told her when she was so happy Raimon had got a place in the orchestra: 'Yes I know you're happy... but don't you worry that he's going to be away travelling a lot?' She'd been so away in the clouds she'd thought Anna was talking about his having an accident. 'No, no,' Anna said, 'I'm talking about him having to stay away overnight... you know what I'm talking about.' Still she went on: 'I'm not afraid of sleeping on my own.' Finally, Anna said: 'Oh, dear, are you so dim? Aren't there any women in the orchestra?'

Blanca had blushed, embarrassed by her naïvety. Yes, there were women in the orchestra, but she'd never imagined Raimon's travelling might cause an extramarital adventure. She allowed Anna to win the day and heard her friend say: 'May the Lord protect you, my child!'

She'd never thought about it again, and was quite happy with it. The position in the orchestra was cause for pure celebration, with no buts. It was what Raimon had wanted for a long time, and when she went to the concert hall and saw him all dressed up in his dark outfit, playing his violin with his eyes closed and the sense of concentration, she was very proud of him. At the end of the day, Anna is very different from her. For a start, she's never been in love with her husband, and she herself recognises this fact. She'd married him kind of out of habit, because they'd been going out for ages, and in all that time she hadn't come across anything better. She loved him, but like a good friend. She didn't desire him, didn't miss him when they were apart, didn't especially admire him either. And most certainly the possibility of cheating on him entered into her calculations. She'd never ruled out the thought of playing away from home if she felt like it one day. 'Your marriage is a different story,' Anna used to tell her. Luckily, Blanca thought.

She definitely had been in love with Raimon when they got married. She still was. Sharing everything with him seemed the most natural thing in the world. They argued, of course, sometimes violently, but there weren't any shadows hanging over their relationship.

Sometimes Anna complained her husband wanted sex too much: 'It's a real drag; if we don't do it every couple of days I get grief. And I hardly ever feel like it...' Blanca restricted herself to smiling understandingly, pretending she shared her friend's revulsion. But she did want to make love very frequently. As often as Raimon did. 'On Saturdays, from the moment I wake up I get myself used to the idea, because I know there's no way I can get away from it,' Anna said. So the last time her friend said she wouldn't mind having a fling, she, Blanca, heard herself saying: 'Yes, right, go and have one, go on. It'll do you good.'

And that's what happened. Anna says she wasn't on the lookout, but the fact is she did find it. 'No, really, all in all very innocent, a few gropes in the lift, that's all.' The thing is, the way she told the story, there seemed nothing sordid about it, just a bit of fun. Raimon had scolded: 'If anybody else but Anna told you the same story you'd be much more critical about it.'

Blanca then thought that when *Forget the Pain* came out in the Catalan translation she'd present a copy to Anna. So she could see how the cookie crumbles when you know you're being deceived.

I'm trying to remember what it was like the first time he told me about her. It must have been the spring of last year, when the last group of interns arrived at the hospital.

As much as I go over it again and again I can't remember. I want to know if he'd told me about these young men and women, if he'd said any were outstanding, if he'd made some throwaway comment about the appearance of the girls. Massimo has always made jokes like that when he sees good-looking women.

I'm preparing the vegetables for dinner and I ask myself time and again; when was the first time he said her name? How come when I first heard him utter it the alarm bells didn't go off inside me? He'll have said 'I was helped by an intern called Isabella,' and I'll have gone on eating or watching the television or playing with the girls, as if nothing had happened. I keep searching on and on through each page of the calendar, and nothing.

What I can establish, on the other hand, is when the suspicion started. I remember because the first time I verbalised it, still jokingly, we were celebrating Flavia's birthday, on the third of September.

My parents and Massimo's were there as well as

12

some of our brothers and sisters. Our little girl was waiting patiently for her father to finish some anecdote from the hospital to blow out the candles on her cake. But he kept on and on, seeing that everyone was laughing their socks off. I could see the wax on the little candles was about to drop off into the icing, and I looked at him purposefully but he just went on and on: '... and then Isabella told the patient to hold his breath while I put the stethoscope on him and the poor man started going redder and redder until Isabella realised and said in all seriousness that he could breathe again if he had to. IF HE HAD TO!'

Flavia was looking at me imploringly, and I interrupted Massimo in a tone which was meant to sound light-hearted: 'That's enough, Massimo, you're always talking about this Isabella... Maybe I'm going to have to start getting jealous.' It wasn't until late in the evening, in bed, that he mentioned her name again: 'Why don't you ever buy nut bread? Isabella brought some in the other day for breakfast and it was really good... I hadn't had any for ages... She says she gets it at the baker's on Via Bagnoli.'

The remark couldn't have been more inoffensive. But I replied, 'See how you talk a lot about this girl?'

Massimo looked at me, as if he were about to laugh. 'Are you jealous? You're jealous!' This amused him because until then he'd always been the one to get jealous. He started tickling me and planting kisses on me and we both laughed. Then he started kissing me and undoing my pyjama top and, I still don't know why, but precisely then I said: 'You mean you don't fancy her?'

The question just came out without a thought.

13

Massimo pulled back and looked at me, his smile still on his lips: 'No, of course not. She's nice, we get on, but that's all.'

I don't remember for sure, but I think we went to sleep that night without making love.

Blanca stopped for a moment to stretch her arms and straighten out her back. Does Raimon talk often about another member of the orchestra? In fact he says little about his colleagues. All he talks about is music. About chords, tempos and symphonies. Who does he have lunch with when he can't get home? He almost never says. Or maybe she never asks. He could quite easily have lunch on his own. He's so withdrawn, Raimon. She, Blanca, often arranges to have lunch with someone. It's the only way to keep relationships healthy: with her sister, her mother, Anna, her nieces.... Her mother used to tell her off sometimes when she called to arrange lunch. 'Why don't you have lunch with Raimon? Have you asked him?' Her mother thought the husband should come before everything. She reminded her that that's how it had been at home growing up: 'For me, as you'll remember, you're father came first of all.' And she, Blanca, would always keep quiet, feeling for her mother and her solitary shut-away widowhood, so different from Sol's.

Her mother a widow, her sister... a widow. No brothers. If it weren't for Raimon, Blanca's close world would be entirely feminine. Raimon provides the counterweight: long silences in the middle of so much conversation, austerity in expressing feelings instead of a festival of hugging and kissing, psychological stability in the face of the switchback ride of female emotions.

After I'd asked if he liked Isabella, I went weeks without thinking about it again. Something inside me had been alerted, but I was still able to think about other things, and this kind of alarm mechanism was only activated by Massimo. And he did it often: he mentioned her by name continually, and recognised openly that they got on really well; he admired her professionally, he always thought her opinion was the right one, she made him laugh.

At that stage I thought that this absence of malice he was exhibiting, talking so openly, was the definitive proof there was nothing to be hidden. At the same time I knew I was becoming an observer, involuntary, but aware of the classic process of falling in love. My husband was falling in love with another woman and I could see him taking one step after another then yet one more.

It must have been then that my self divided into two Brunas: one Bruna in love with Massimo, blindly trusting in him, dismissing suspicion and keeping faith in a relationship I felt was solid and stable, and the Bruna in love with Massimo who sensed, with a shocking certainty, that her love was crumbling and Massimo would escape through the cracks and there was nothing she could do about it, a Bruna going a bit crazier every day. The two Brunas confronted each other, fought and sometimes insulted each other (How can you be so naïve? How can you be so distrustful? Massimo is NOT like the rest of them! Massimo IS like every other man!). Often the sage Bruna would win: Isabella was a friendly, smart girl and Massimo thought she was an excellent work colleague, and certainly she got his hormones up with her flirting. There isn't anything wrong in that.

That was the very expression Massimo kept repeating over those months, as I was starting to complain, question, suspect. 'I'm not doing anything wrong.' Then there was a ticking off: 'What's the matter? Aren't I allowed to have any friends?' He said this because for years he'd been so dedicated to his medical training, and then his work at the hospital, that he didn't actually have many, friends that is. I'd always been careful to maintain relationships and often went out to dinner with people from work, the mothers from school, old friends.... Could that be it? Could it be that from there on I wouldn't be the only important person in Massimo's life, his single pillar of affection?

He kept saying 'I'm not doing anything wrong', his fortress-phrase where he probably hid himself from what he was doing. Gradually, very gradually, I was withering. Massimo lived by my side but didn't see me, like a faded rose in some forgotten pot in the corner, where no one remembered to water it, or even throw it out with the rubbish.

Slowly I ceased to live the relatively happy life I had been building over the last few years. I lost my sense of humour, patience and energy. The only feeling I was sure of was that I was in the way.

Sometimes, when he was on call several times in a row, I missed him. I missed the Massimo I loved, the one who surely no longer existed. Around then I'd leave a piece of paper for him, next to the coffee machine, with a note: 'I miss you. What about having lunch together today? Can you find a moment to get away?'

It's true that most times this happened Massimo did

have lunch with me. And he'd tell me off for not being happy enough. 'Isn't this what you wanted?'

No, it wasn't what I wanted. To begin with, I wanted him to be the one who made the suggestion, for him to miss me too, and say so. In any event I'd have liked him to accept my proposal happily and not with resignation: 'I've got lots of work to do and a meeting first thing in the afternoon, but I'll try and find space,' in that desultory tone as if he was doing it because he had to.

Another change I couldn't avoid and which ate away at my state of mind was that I stopped feeling at ease around town. Taormina, where I was born, the town I love, ceased to welcome me. Strolling through its streets became a torment rather than a pleasure. It caused me great anguish and took me a little while to work out why. It was one day as I was looking in the shop windows on Corso Umberto. I realised that before I stopped to look I glanced inside the shop, and went straight past the cafés without looking in the windows. All of a sudden I stopped and put my hand to my chest. My heart was going so fast it frightened me. I realised what the thought was that caused me all these physical reactions: I'm afraid, I thought. And of what? The answer presented itself all on its own: running into them.

By this point my life was filled with suspicion but still nothing was certain. Massimo and a couple of my friends I'd mentioned things to made me out to be hysterical and neurotic. Deep down I hoped they all were right. But deeper still, I knew I wasn't wrong, and that one day I might see them in the street, or sitting in a café, or driving around in our car. And this image terrified me. I stopped walking *through Taormina. I went from home to school and from school to home. I didn't feel at liberty to do anything, was scared, insecure, and didn't know who I was.*

That evening Blanca welcomed Raimon home with a lavish dinner, smoked salmon and white wine chilling in the fridge. He knew there didn't need to be any celebration required for a dinner like this. His wife did it from time to time, for no particular reason. She also gave him presents when it wasn't necessary, or she'd surprise him on the most unexpected evening in a special set of lingerie.

That night, however, there was a reason, although Blanca didn't realise. She'd prepared this dinner out of a need, not yet fully defined, to create an intimate atmosphere. She wasn't aware of it, but deep down all the preparations were directed towards facilitating the right ambience in which to pose a question: have you ever been unfaithful to me?

Raimon spluttered on his wine. They were talking about how they'd met. The conversation, started by Blanca, had flowed smoothly as far as remembering old relationships. When she brought up the name of someone at university she'd had a fleeting adventure with, Raimon's face suddenly changed.

'But Raimon... that was ten years ago and I wasn't going out with you then!'

'I'm not jealous, but you know that idiot has always really irritated me. He's a waste of space and I can't understand how you got involved with him.'

Blanca knew she was treading on dangerous ground. A few times before this conversation had ended up badly, but she took the risk.

'You had something going with that girl who lived in your

parents' block when I met you.... Don't say you didn't...'

'What's that got to do with anything?'

Raimon looked at her, uneasily, and she found him irresistible with that expression.

She went to him and sat on his lap, straddling him, and put her hands round his neck. As she stroked him, she looked him in the eyes and put the question:

'Have you ever been unfaithful to me?' She noticed Raimon's almost imperceptible pout. Then a broad smile opened up and looking at her straight he said to her, 'Of course not, you know that.'

It was a comforting evening. They made love enthusiastically, amid laughter. But when Raimon went to sleep eventually, clasping her from behind, Blanca took some time to fall into slumber. She was sure she'd seen that ever so slight movement when she'd asked the question. She dreamt she woke Raimon suddenly, shone a bright light into his eyes and asked him the question over and over again. He always answered 'Of course not, you know that', but each time there was an involuntary movement of a muscle somewhere in his body. She didn't rest at all.

My mother started to notice something was happening to me. She looked at me inquisitorially, called me at odd times and asked me questions out of the blue. I did the best I could to pretend nothing was going on, but with little hope of success, because if there's any absolute truth in our relationship it's that my mother can see straight through me. She can work out what's going on with me as easily as she can do a child's jigsaw puzzle. She just has to look at the pieces for a moment and in a blink of an eye move them from one place to another and they all fit together.

Today she's come to meet me after school as a surprise. I come out with the girls and see her sitting on a bench in the square, fidgeting and looking around at nothing in particular. When she sees me she attempts a nonchalant smile.

'I'm inviting you to tea.'

Her news is greeted with squeals from the girls, who hug her so tightly they almost knock her off balance.

'Do you mind me coming without saying?'

I mind that she always thinks I mind.

'Why should I mind? It's a lovely surprise.... But is there any special reason you've come?'

'You see, Bruna? You're so.... Aren't I allowed to want to have tea with my daughter and grandchildren?'

'Of course you are Mum, of course you are....'

When Flavia and Giulia had finished their hot chocolate they went out to play on the swings and my mother and I were left alone in the cafeteria with a cappucino in front of each of us and an uncomfortable silence over the table.

'Are you going to tell me what's up, Bruna?'

My mother's voice sounds affectionate for the moment.

'Nothing at all, don't worry. I'm getting my period and I'm tired.'

'You're always getting your period when I ask you if anything's wrong.'

'I get it quite often, Mum. Once a month to be precise.'

'If you're going to get sarcastic we might as well give up.'

I finish my cappuccino and apologise. I suddenly feel an urgent need to get home, take off my clothes and shoes, maybe have a very hot shower and get into my pyjamas...

'Shall we go?'

'There's something I wanted to ask... I hope you don't mind...'

'Go on.'

'Your marriage... is it all right?'

She knows me. She works me out. It makes me mad. I shut up.

'I knew it! You've fallen in love with somebody else, haven't you? I knew it! So silent, so withdrawn!'

Without looking up, I start smiling. I laugh freely and with a readiness I haven't felt for days. My mother thinks I've got a lover! The idea makes me laugh, but at the bottom of it all there's the same telling off as ever. She doesn't trust me. She thinks it'll all turn out bad and it'll all be my fault. My eyes fill with tears.

She looks at me, distressed, and strokes my hand.

'I'm sorry, Mum. Rest assured that there's nothing wrong. I'm just tired, I promise.'

We go out onto the street arm in arm. I wish I could tell her the whole story. That Massimo has fallen in love with someone else, or at least that's what I suspect. That I've been living in torment for months, my life is getting darker, dirtier, more unbearable by the day. I wish I could unburden myself, and that my mother could just hug me, console me, protect me. But that's never happened and won't happen now. My mother challenges me, judges me, cross-examines me. She doesn't rest until she's found the best in me. Her demand is unlimited, prodding, exhausting.

It's twelve noon. The sun floods into Blanca's study. She looks at the photograph she has pinned up on the corkboard in front of her. Her mother and her hugging each other, looking into the lens with an almost identical smile. They look so much alike. The same mouth. Would she talk to her, she to her mother, if she thought she'd fallen for another man, or if she believed Raimon was being unfaithful?

They've always had an excellent relationship. She's always thought she could tell her everything, but up till now obviously there's never been anything to be secretive about in her life. When she started going out with Raimon, she kept her up to date with the whole story without a second thought. She did it naturally, as she always had, and she'd never spent five minutes valuing this good relationship in her life. She took it as a given. Her mother understood her, consoled her, and listened to her whenever it was necessary. She never demanded explanations, never demanded anything. It was as if her mother had taken her role to be a passive one, simply that of a receiver. Maybe now she thinks about it, possibly a bit too much. Maybe she occasionally would have liked her mother to have given her a grilling, made her reconsider a decision carefully, or argued over something. All the same... she feels compassion for Bruna.

Everybody needs consoling. 'Consol': she's got it twice! Her mother's name is Consol and her sister too, Consol, Sol.

It's true that sometimes she gets treated as if she were still a child. It's the younger sister syndrome, and whatever age you are you're the one who needs protecting. At home it was all reinforced when her father died. Her mother and Sol enveloped the adolescent and vulnerable Blanca, and since then it's been difficult to correct the clichés. She isn't an adolescent any more, and is sure she's less vulnerable, but they still protect her, and sometimes she thinks this protection acts as a brake, making her fearful.

She also acknowledges that such a tight bond of trust with her mother and sister, which normally is so comforting, can sometimes – just sometimes – feel a little smothering. Occasionally she feels she's too transparent, and that her mother and sister know everything about her, so nothing is purely hers. As if she longs for a secret she's never had. Raimon does keep some feelings hidden. Nothing major, for sure, but there is a corner somewhere in him where nobody goes. Not even Blanca. Far from troubling her, she's always found this attractive: as they say, opposite poles attract. She's an open book and he's mysterious.

Raimon is a man of long silences and Blanca is always talking. He's shy and reserved, she's outgoing and communicative.

All of a sudden she now remembers – she'd never given it a second thought – the moment when she told her sister she was falling in love with Raimon. Sol hadn't yet met him and asked what he was like. Blanca said: 'He's got a very gentle look about him, but one which hides mystery. He keeps quiet, and I like the contrast, because I sometimes talk too much'.

Sol then said to her: 'Don't let yourself be dazzled by mystery. Sometimes when people are quiet it's because they have nothing to say.'

Just imagine, remembering that sentence now, which Sol said when she hadn't even met him.... What does she think now, Sol, about Raimon? They have a cordial relationship, affectionate Blanca would say, but... she'll ask her.

Secretly, Blanca has always thought her sister has turned her lost husband into a mythical figure and since then hasn't found any man to be near his equal. That's why she's never found another stable relationship since Jaume died. In fact Sol recognises this: 'It's very difficult to find the person you can, and want to, share your life with. I found that person once, and it's unlikely I'll have the same luck again.'

When her sister uses the word 'luck' she doesn't know whether to laugh or cry. The man she loved, the father of her children, left home one bright December morning to climb to the top of a mountain. He was taken by surprise by a sudden snowstorm and when they found him the next day he was already dead. He was twenty-nine years old.

A very strong wind has got up, and the branches of the neighbours' almond tree, full to bursting of white, are dancing. 'It's come out too early,' thinks Blanca. She's afraid the blossom will all be blown away. There have been some very good days and the almond has been hard at work, but we're only getting into February. Sometimes life gets ahead of itself.

Chapter Two

It started getting dark early. Coming out of school with the girls we went straight home, not stopping at the park because it was cold. The afternoons were getting longer, for me, and I felt caged in. The prospect of a long dull winter was painful, and I couldn't see any chink which might allow light into my cage.

As I gave Flavia and Giulia their supper, I worked hard at being happy, made them laugh with some story or other and listened as they recounted endless tales of playground scraps and what they'd done at school. I can be happy, I kept telling myself. Nothing has changed, yet: I have a husband and two children who I love, and who love me, our life is reasonably pleasant, I have a job which is sometimes satisfying, I live in a beautiful, fun town, I have good friends.... But I always end up looking at the clock: it's late, he should be home by now.

I was telling myself not to get worked up. I wanted to keep my good mood going for when Massimo got home, welcome him with a smile and a hug, present the perfect picture of a warm family in a comfortable home.

But Massimo got home very late. He came in looking tired and muttering excuses about the traffic and a last-minute emergency case. The kids threw themselves on him, kissing him all over and taking his attention. I wanted him for me. I wanted him to hold me, ask me how I was, and immediately I found myself in self-recrimination: how could I be jealous of my own daughters? Eventually, after a useless struggle with my suspicions and horrible thoughts, my positive mood deserted me and when we sat down to dinner I had to fight to give an appearance of normality.

So forcing a light-hearted tone, I asked him how his day had been and he told me little stories from the hospital; his day seemed interesting, fun, fullfilling, and when he asked 'What about you?' I searched for a way to hide the boredom of my classes, playing with the girls, making dinner, ironing.

Massimo told me, affectionately, that I looked unhappy and tired. Why don't you do something a bit different? Call a friend and go out for dinner, buy yourself something nice to wear. I looked at him from my abyss and he was ever further away. I don't want to go for dinner with friends. I don't want to buy a new dress. I want you.

Blanca imagined Massimo to be very good-looking, a bit like George Clooney. Bruna can't be a great beauty, but'll be a good-hearted girl, probably light-eyed, slim and not very tall. Like them, she thinks immediately. In other words an attractive man and an ordinary woman. Sometimes she sees this in the eyes of people who ask themselves what he could possibly see in her, he's such a gorgeous, interesting man. She mentions this to him, half joking, half serious, and he tells her off. 'I don't want you saying that. That's a load of rubbish.' But he never adds anything caring. He's very sparing with words. It's a big effort for him to say she has lovely eyes or she looks great in that outfit. Sometimes Blanca thinks he'll end up speaking only through music.

When he plays his violin, at home and just for her, the melody sometimes becomes all the romantic words Raimon never utters. Blanca feels his fingers gently stroking the strings as if they were playing her skin. The movement of the bow is an embrace and the pressure of his chin on the instrument makes her imagine the caresses even more deeply.

When the music comes to an end, Raimon remains a few seconds with the violin to his face, eyes closed, the sound of the melody within him. He then delicately lays the instrument in its case, takes her hand and leads her to the bed. He undresses her, runs his hands all over her, makes her tremble and quiver.

If Blanca suspected Raimon's hands could touch another body with that same tenderness, the same desire, the pain would be unbearable, devastating. She's never thought of herself as jealous, but Bruna's story has found its way into her mind and she can imagine her suffering perfectly.

She's talked to her sister a few times about unfaithfulness. Sol, as always, has some odd ideas: unfaithfulness without feeling, only for sex, can be forgiven, she says roundly. Blanca disagrees. Sol comes back with: 'If you love someone and that person loves you, a purely sexual transgression is an obviously unpleasant incident, but it's just an anecdotal event.' Sol, since she plunged into the abyss, sees everything from up on high, as if nothing affects her and never could: sexual infidelity has no importance. It's not very nice but you can get over it.

Put like that it looks as if she's right, but if you picture the writhing naked bodies it all gets a bit more complicated. 'Bruna,' thinks Blanca, 'you're unnerving me,' and she turns off the computer. She's done enough for today. She'll go and get dressed then turn up and surprise Raimon when he comes out of rehearsal.

She chooses dark trousers, a pale woollen jumper and a light jacket. She puts on a little eyeliner and ties her hair back the way her husband likes it.

She arrives at the concert hall impatient to see him and asks at reception. The concierge informs her that the rehearsal finished early and all the musicians have left. There's no one left in the building.

She goes out and hails a taxi. She's anxious to get home and see if Raimon's there. 'Why does he have such a thing about not having a mobile,' she protests to herself.

When she puts the key in the lock and finds out he has already got home she finds herself calming down. What was she thinking? That he wasn't going to be there? Where was Raimon going to go, at nine o'clock in the evening, without her? And anyway, so what if he *had* gone somewhere? Raimon comes out of the bathroom and hugs her. She gives him a long kiss. It's so good you're here at home. After dinner they sit for a while in the little music room. It's not a big room, and one day it'll be their first son's or daughter's. At the moment there's a quality hi-fi system installed and a storage unit for Raimon's hundreds of CDs. There are two armchairs, a standard lamp and a small bookcase. It's a good refuge in which to take shelter at the end of the day. Raimon chooses the music – Bach, Mahler, or Pachelbel – and sits in one of the armchairs. He leans his head back and closes his eyes. Blanca sits in the other armchair with the novel she's currently reading. Occasionally she becomes submerged in the story imprisoned in the pages, but most often she watches Raimon. The calmness of his face, his features softened by the pleasure of the music. Until this evening she'd never thought these moments of peace could ever actually disappear. Maybe one day she'll find unease building within her and won't be able to enjoy watching Raimon's closed eyes, his body relaxed in the chair, his fingers dancing on his thigh as he follows the harmonies. Perhaps the day will come when she won't be able to look at him without asking herself questions, or reproaching him and opening up old wounds. The melody cradles her in its arms as she formulates a little prayer to herself that it never ever happens.

Next day she was anxious to get down to work. She wanted to know what happened to Bruna. It was as if an old friend was having a tough time and she wanted to call to see how things were going. It took her no effort at all to imagine Bruna's voice on the phone, a velvety voice, a little darkened. For God's sake, it was as if she really knew her.

Before she went back to *Forget the Pain*, she opened the web browser and typed Taormina.

She knew it was in north-east Sicily, a town very popular with tourists and surrounded by wonderful countryside which had been turned into the chosen haven of aristocrats, artists, and multi-millionaires from all over Europe.

As she looks at the photographs of different parts of the

town, Blanca finds it hard to believe how anyone who lives in Taormina could be unhappy. Does living in a pretty place make life more pleasant? Would she be happier living in an attic in Paris, a little house with a garden in the middle of Amsterdam, or an old castle in Scotland surrounded by fields and meadows whose greenness is only lost in the far distance?

Without her meaning to, she lets her gaze escape towards the almond tree in next door's yard. In the middle of the city, with the noise, the dirt, the crowds of people, that almond is her only clear link with nature. From her February window, with spring nowhere to be seen, Blanca senses the future of fine weather, clear skies and long days. A patch of hope. She would like Bruna to have a blossoming almond nearby.

At Christmas we spent a few days in Naples, at Massimo's parents'. The girls were dying to see their grandparents, and especially loved playing with their cousins. I was also very glad to leave Taormina for a few days. I felt that leaving the town would help me get away from my obsessions, and above all I had the burning desire that Massimo not go to the hospital, in other words not see Isabella.

Naples welcomed us as always with a burst of life. Massimo's parents and brothers and sisters allowed me to rediscover the man with whom I'd fallen in love, free of the trappings of his prestige as a surgeon. In Naples he enjoyed eating his mother's ricotta ravioli and drinking Malvasia, meeting old friends who bore no resemblance to his work colleagues, and, as far as I was concerned, being much more devoted to me.

On Christmas night, at dinner with his parents and surrounded by brothers and sisters, including in-laws, and nephews, bachelor uncles and toddler cousins, Massimo took hold of my hand under the table. I was as thrilled as if it were the very first time he'd done it, and clasped his hand in mine. He smiled at me and moved his lips silently to say 'I love you'.

I felt like telling everyone to stop talking, getting up on my chair and shouting: Massimo loves me! You see? It was all a figment of my imagination. Massimo isn't having an affair with anyone. Massimo loves me!

That night I slept soundly and when I woke the next morning I rushed to hug Flavia and Giulia, in a state of euphoria with my fantastic family. I felt like saying to Massimo: 'See how easy it was to make me happy?'

We returned to Taormina relaxed and reconciled. He with me. Me with life. For four or five weeks it seemed everything was going back to normal. I was able to become interested in his work again and not doubt he was telling the truth when he was late home. One day I told him I was going to the psychiatrist. He was surprised but didn't say anything.

'Is there anything wrong with that?' I asked him.

'No, not at all. It's just I thought you were better and didn't need to any more.'

'You don't understand, Massimo. Of course I'm better. I now believe my jealousy was completely unfounded, and that means I have a problem to resolve. I don't want it to happen ever again, not with Isabella or anyone else.'

I was quite frankly pleased to have taken this decision, although I was aware Massimo didn't seem convinced at all. I thought maybe he was afraid the climate we'd enjoyed since Christmas might be damaged.

To me, though, it was very clear I needed help and I sought it.

Going to the psychiatrist every fortnight was a financial burden, a headache to fit into my hectic schedule, and above all a source of anguish: I've never been thrilled at the idea of revealing my intimate thoughts to a stranger, and even less so when I feel ashamed of them, as was the case here. I left each session exhausted and planned secretly not to return, but as the days passed I forced myself to, mainly because deep down I was sure I hadn't overcome my obsessions.

Massimo was very tired. There'd been a lot of work at the hospital and he was sleeping badly. So when he told me he wanted to go to a weekend conference in Palermo it seemed a good opportunity for him to have a change and a rest. We were coming up to the date and I didn't dare ask the question which had my stomach in knots, removing my appetite completely.

Finally, the night before he left, as he was packing his suitcase with a diligence I'd never seen before, I asked, as if casually: 'Which of you are going to this conference then?'

Massimo had his back to me and I saw the muscles in his neck tauten.

'Oh, about eight or nine of us are going.'

I instantly knew she was one of the eight or nine. Was he going to make me ask? No. He took pity on me and said: 'Yes... Isabella is going. It's perfectly logical, it's what she's specialised in. Don't get wound up, okay?'

Don't get wound up? My stomach, where this wretched question had been, was suddenly flooded by butterflies which didn't stop moving the entire weekend.

Massimo called me loads of times. Each time the phone rang I wiped away the tears, took a deep breath and tried to hide the sobs in my voice. He, however, was serious and made it clear, without saying so, that I was spoiling the conference for him. I felt jealous, sad, guilty, furious, and alone.
And the butterflies churned up more than ever.

Blanca feels the heat of the coffee in her hand and the cold of the glass on her forehead. She likes the contrast. She could spend all morning like this: her hands holding the steaming cup and her head resting on the window. The sky is pure white today. A milky light envelopes everything and the outlines of the buildings seem less defined.

She has a slight headache. As if this whiteness of the sky weighs too much. Life in the city seems half stopped. The branches of the almond are still, there are no birds around to flit across the view from the window, not even the washing hung out on the balconies is moving. And the sky is ever denser.

All of a sudden Blanca sees a fleck of whiter light, glinting as it falls rapidly before her eyes. It's a minute snowflake. Her eyes follow it. Then another. And another. It's snowing and life goes on out there. White snow on the white blossom of the almond tree. A wonder.

Blanca wants it to snow more, and for the snow to be whiter. For the window to get colder still. The coffee darker and hotter. She wouldn't move from where she is for anything in the world. The roofs are turning white and the picture of the city, so very dull recently, gradually turns unreal, spectacular.

An expert voice on the radio tells her the weather front will cover the whole country. Temperatures are falling, roads getting blocked, and there's snow even at the beach.

She's always been excited by these exceptional situations of relative emergency.

She likes lightning storms and thunder, when gales blow up angrily over the hills, when the lights go out. It all reminds her fondly of when she was little, at her grandparents' house up in Empordà.

The wind whistling and the shutters banging, big raindrops against the window panes, fluorescent lights flickering until they went out, thunderclaps. And she sitting on the floor in front of the fire, by her grandfather's chair. Each time the wind howled she felt his enormous hand on her head. She's never felt so protected again since then.

Now, as the snow falls gently and wraps the country in white cellophane, she wraps herself up in that scene of her grandpa gently stroking her curly hair with his broad open hand, the wind outside screaming down from the mountains but without a hope of scaring her.

She has only ever managed to come close to this feeling when Raimon strokes her hair, gently, after making love to her.

When Massimo returned from the conference I watched and watched him, trying to find in his body the telltale signs of infidelity. I felt that somehow those beloved eyes, those longed-for hands, would uncover the secret for me. My Massimo, the man I'd loved for so many years I'd lost count, wouldn't be able to hide from me that he'd made love with a woman other than myself.

'What are you looking at?' he said, disconcerted.

'I'm looking at you,' I replied unflinching. His eyes turned away and he chewed his bottom lip.

During the weekend of the conference I'd imagined several times the scene of his return, when he sat me down, still with his jacket on, and said 'We have to talk...' or 'There's something I have to tell you.' I could almost hear the words, and it was as if I were standing on scaffolding, someone moving the planks to make me lose my balance. There was nothing for me to grab hold of and I couldn't help but fall.

I did try and redirect these negative thoughts as the psychiatrist had told me to. I told myself that if Massimo was the scaffolding I'd climbed on to for survival there were other things to hold on to so as not to fall if he failed me: my daughters, my job, my friends, my family, myself. I forced myself to believe that if Massimo left me I would not fall.

But Massimo came back from the conference and didn't say anything out of the ordinary.

'It went well, but I didn't have any time to rest or enjoy myself – it was all lectures and workgroups...'

The psychiatrist had recommended I 'open up the conflict'. He recommended I didn't shut away my obsessions in a little box inside me where they would go mouldy and putrefy. Whatever it took, I had to open the box and release the obsessions, make them public, give them air. That way I would continually diminish them until they went drifting away out of the window, the same way as when little children blow at dandelion clocks.

I started to think about which of the people close to me could become my confidante. It was a disappointing exercise. The first five names on the list were soon crossed off: my mother – she'd find a way of making me feel guilty;

my two sisters – Paola for being too cautious, Cecilia for being too harsh; my brother Guido because he was a long way away; and my friend Ida – to avoid the whole of Taormina from buzzing with my anxieties. In actual fact I knew exactly who I wanted to share this with, the person with whom I'd always shared everything, Massimo, the only person who couldn't listen to me.

I wished I could duplicate him, clone him, have a Massimo of my own, the old one, who I could go to for solace in the face of the other Massimo's cruelty. It was indeed a little bit like that: some nights, in bed in the dark, when he hugged me close and silently, I felt Massimo was the old one, my one.

It's curious. During the day, Massimo was much clearer. He denied my accusations explicitly and in a raised tone of voice: I AM NOT BEING UNFAITHFUL TO YOU WITH ISABELLA. I AM NOT HAVING AN AFFAIR. On the other hand there was much more sincerity in his silences in the night, in the tightness of his hugs in the dark.

Blanca can't help thinking about who she would confide in if she found herself in Bruna's situation. She puts together a list in her mind and breathes out in relief: fortunately she wouldn't have trouble choosing someone to turn to. Straight off there are four who come to mind, four female names: Consol, her mother; Consol, her sister; Anna, her friend; and Violeta, Raimon's sister.

In fact, gaping differences aside, it would be a relief to be able to explain to one of these four people the minuscule concern which had lodged inside her since the night she asked her husband if he'd ever been unfaithful. The strange expression on Raimon's face, which she'd attributed to surprise, while a wicked little voice murmured in her ear: maybe it wasn't surprise, maybe he was afraid you'd suspect something, afraid you'd uncover a secret of his.

She knows she has to verbalise her fears if she wants to minimise them. Bruna's psychiatrist is right: if she shuts them away inside her they'll end up growing and building. Does she really think her husband is cheating on her, or is capable of ever doing so? She picks up the phone and starts dialling her mother's home number... but she stops halfway through. Would she be able to make her mother understand that all she wanted was to say her suspicion out loud so as to neutralise it? She'd overreact with worry. She imagines her calling constantly, peppering her with questions, worrying about her at all hours and turning Raimon into a criminal without any evidence. She decides to think carefully about who she wants to talk to before dialling any numbers. Almost without realising, she's ruled out Raimon's sister. Violeta and Blanca have had an extremely friendly relationship ever since the beginning but... from that to making her into the person she trusts over uneasiness concerning her brother.... She knows Raimon very well and her opinion would be valuable... but no, no.

What about Anna? Anna has kept their secrets since they were little. She's her oldest friend and must be her best. They've talked about boys and falling in love since they've had the use of reason, and she's the ideal person to have a spicy superficial conversation with. But if Blanca confessed her fears to her, what would Anna say? 'He probably is being unfathful, they all do it. So what? Let him enjoy himself... that's the stuff of life. You should do the same yourself.' No, no. She needs someone who talks the same language as her.

37

She phones Sol. Sol does exactly what Blanca thought she would. She's not especially surprised, but she calms her down. She takes the drama out of the conversation but doesn't take it all too lightly.

Her sister maintains that while a sexual infidelity is not pleasant it can't destroy a relationship. Love, friendship, sharing and mutual respect are worth a thousand times more than a moment of weakness. In any event Sol doesn't think for a minute Raimon would be capable of betraying her. It's ridiculous. How can anyone allow themselves to be influenced by a novel to such an extent?

After their conversation and much more relaxed, Blanca again felt she wished she could call Bruna. She wanted to tell her that it really wasn't that easy to find someone suitable to confide in. She, who'd always felt she had solid friendships around her, had also discarded the names of some very close people. But she has her sister. She has Sol.

That evening it snows again. In mid afternoon the sky darkens all of a sudden and the snow begins to fall in slow motion. She rolls down the blinds to keep the flat warm and lies down on the bed and waits for Raimon. She can hear the wind blowing outside and an unfamiliar shiver runs down her spine. Her eyes closed, she curls and wraps her arms around herself as if to protect her belly, in which a tiny fear has taken root, an almost imperceptible tremble. She would give anything for her grandfather's protecting hand on her head now. Raimon wakens her with kisses on her hair. Those beloved dark eyes. How could she have thought he might hurt her?

She falls asleep in the cradle of Raimon's eyes and dreams of Bruna high on an unsteady platform, desperately trying to find something to grab on to and keep from falling. Like a film, the camera tracks upwards to the top of the building where a man's hands are shaking the ropes on which the platform is suspended.

Alla fine di ottobre... At the end of October I was walking through the centre of Taormina with my colleague Oriana and twenty-five seven and eight year old boys and girls, our schoolchildren. We were going to the Palazzo Corvaja and the Greek Theatre, two of the town's main monuments.

I wished I had more than two eyes to keep track of all the children. They were walking in pairs, holding hands, and behaving really quite well, but experience told me I had to watch them carefully: at any moment they might stop in front of a shop window and everyone would be held up, or they'd step off the pavement totally unexpectedly.

We were just coming into Piazza Vittorio Emanuele, where the palace is, when I saw Massimo, out of the corner of my eye, on the far side of the square. He was standing still and appeared to be waiting for someone. In a flash the children disappeared, as did the traffic in the square, the pedestrians, the noise, the whole of Taormina. Stock still, paralysed, I watched the scene as if I were in a cinema, in the dark, transfixed by the screen.

A girl with dark wavy hair came out of a tobacconist's, went up to him, and the two began to walk, side by side. They were talking, looking at each other, smiling freely. I was standing there motionless, in the middle of the street, watching them. The children went past me, laughing and screeching, and Oriana called out: 'Bruna! Bruna! What on earth are you stopping for?' Everything carried on functioning around me but it was as if someone had turned my power switch off.

Massimo and the girl went out of sight. I hadn't seen them kiss, or touch, or even take each other's hand to cross the road. Nevertheless I was absolutely certain it was Isabella and that there was something going on between them.

Oriana had to come up and shake me gently. 'Bruna...' I started walking on instinct alone; my legs felt like rubber, not responding properly. All the noise of the street rang around in my head and I struggled to find any sensible words.

'Let's go,' I said. 'I was feeling a bit faint.'

A friendly young man was waiting for us at the Palazzo Corvaja and he explained how the decorative motifs of the façade were made of lava from Mount Etna and... I followed the group, concentrating all my efforts on trying to hide the fact my body was trembling.

It's very difficult to explain, even to myself, but the fact of the matter is although I had no proof, and despite not having witnessed any compromising behaviour, my vision of Massimo at that moment dispelled all my doubts. I knew that he, the man I loved, was at that instant another woman's man.

I didn't know if he was in love or simply in lust. I didn't know if she felt the same for him, or not. I didn't know if they were lovers or just flirting. But I recognised perfectly the way Massimo was. It was the way he wasn't with me any more.

I went back to the school with Oriana and the children and when we got there I went straight to the headmaster's office to apologise. I wasn't feeling well, I'd felt faint in the middle of the street and probably hadn't paid enough attention to the children. I was going to go home and call the doctor.

I cried all the way, furiously wiping away the tears with the palms of my hands and praying I didn't bump into anyone I knew. I didn't call the doctor. I called Massimo.

'I saw you in Piazza Vittorio Emanuele, at midday.'

There was so much accusation in the sentence I even scared myself.

Massimo flew off the handle immediately and started yelling. He said he was coming home and hung up the phone. He was incandescent.

I got into bed and pulled the bedclothes over my head. I wanted to disappear, spare myself the scene to come. I wanted to die.

I heard the key in the lock and the door closing loudly. His purposeful steps and the bedroom door opening.

'Bruna.'

There wasn't a single grain of affection in his voice as he said my name. He had said it so many times with love, with desire, with respect.

'I can't take this any more.'

The fury had gone. He took on the part of the victim but at the same time looked at me compassionately. He waited for me to speak but I had nothing to say. There was no rational logic. I knew I had no arguments, that I couldn't convince him that quite simply my heart was telling me something and I believed it.

'I guess there's nothing I can say.... You can see that yourself. You can't control your own actions any more and I can't take it.'

He was the victim.

'I've really tried to be patient... I've... I've always loved you very much.... But I won't put up with you spying on me. I'm a grown man and it doesn't say anywhere that I belong to you or that you can control me. I haven't done anything wrong. You've seen me in the street with someone from work. Great. And? You think I was wrong to be there? I'm sorry, I thought we could work all of this out, I thought the psychiatrist was going to be able to help you, but...'

I stayed silent. There was nothing I could say. Inside me there was just a huge emptiness and a dark silence. I remembered only one of all the sentences he'd said: I've always loved you very much, I've always loved you very much.

Massimo came close and kissed my forehead. 'I don't want to live like this another day, Bruna.'

I saw him leaving the room and the earth opened slowly beneath me. I was falling. Falling. Until I found the strength to say:

'Massimo.'

He turned and for a couple of seconds I thought I glimpsed a little bit of love in his eyes. That was enough. I had to hang on to that to stop me falling. I wanted to ask him if he loved me. If he loved Isabella. If he wanted to leave me for her. If he wanted to stay with me. But all I said was, 'I'm sorry.'

He nodded his head. Tired. Horribly tired. And he left.

It doesn't say anywhere that I belong to you, Massimo had said. And he was right. I'd always felt the

42

same way about love. I believed in individual freedom and respect. I didn't like people who were possessive and would never tolerate anyone who tried to control me.... So? Why were these words so hurtful? It must have been because deep down inside I felt that I did belong to Massimo. After so many years living so close to him, how he looked at me, held me... I belonged to him. And didn't he belong to me a little bit? Perhaps he did, but not to the point where I could go spying on his daily existence, or stop him from doing something or other, or demanding explanations. He was right.

He came back home late, when the girls were already in bed. I waited for him on the sofa, with the lights down low so as to hide the redness of my eyes. I wanted to present an image of serenity. I needed to restore to myself a little dignity and had worked out a long long speech, which fell apart in the first sentence. All I managed was to ask him not to lie to me. 'If you've fallen in love, I know there's nothing I can do about it. But don't deceive me. I need to be able to respect you. You're the father of my children.'

His eyes were already giving off sparks when I stopped. He didn't say anything. Not a word.

He turned around and went into the bedroom and I was left there alone, in a daze, as if everything around me was falling apart

The man with whom I shared my life and my children was capable of leaving me alone, fighting with my desperation, without a word or touch to console me. Was he even unable to sit beside me silently just so I wasn't alone? Would he be able to go to sleep, knowing that I was *in torment just a few yards away? That night I realised he would never convince me. Massimo didn't love me any more. I only had to try and decide if I felt able to live without him.*

What about having a baby? It's an idea she's dismissed out of hand up to now but today she wants to think about it for a moment. She goes over and over it, and concludes that what is pushing her that way is fear. She's afraid of losing Raimon – Sol was hurt by death, Bruna by betrayal – and thinks that if she had a child of her own, of the two of them, it would be like never losing him completely. Is that a good reason for having a baby? Are there good and bad reasons for wanting to be a mother?

Why is she thinking about rescuing herself from something dreadful which she hasn't yet suffered and maybe never will? And why should she need saving from it? It's true a tragedy like her sister's is very rare, but there are loads of broken marriages every single day. She reads about them in magazines, and her friends are forever saying so and so have split up. A few months later it's: You know that one? She's living with that other bloke. And her ex, he's moved in with a woman who only got separated a couple of months ago.

Blanca isn't sure whether to just relax – after all you can get over a separation relatively easily and you fall in love with someone else pretty soon really – or whether she should start thinking she's a bit special (nothing more precise, just leave it at 'special'). Much of the time she thinks most people generally are like her friend Anna: who they love is in fact an accident of circumstance. The same as their job, or the flat they live in. Sometimes you have to move and it doesn't have to be such a drama. I'll live in this flat while it suits me; a bit like that.

She believes Raimon is the spinal column of her life. That without Raimon she wouldn't be Blanca. That's why the thought of losing him makes her feel ill. She is certain that his love is for always. And she likes it like that, but has these little panic attacks when among her thoughts the question crops up: does Raimon see things exactly the same way?

A few months ago, there was only one possible answer. Blanca had always taken it as a given. In fact, though, had Raimon ever actually said it? Sol has told her many times you can't take anything as a given, not even the very fact of living.

Blanca stops her brooding like someone putting on the handbrake in a car. Let's see: her mother, a sensitive, not especially brave woman, was able to overcome her father's death a few years ago; her sister was able to cope with the tragedy of the death of her young husband, with whom she was very much in love, and the horror of being left on her own with two young kids; so Blanca then, an intelligent and independent woman, she'd be able to manage without Raimon. Of course she could! Or not?

There are many things we are capable of, and don't realise until we have to do them. We don't know ourselves well enough to predict how we'll behave in extreme situations. Neither do we know what causes us to act in a certain way, rather than some other. Bravery or fear? Generosity or egotism? Considered thought or recklessness? She, Blanca, can she be sure she loves Raimon with generosity and nobility? Or does she love him with selfishness and fear? How did they reach the commitment to share each other's lives? Responsibly or impulsively?

If Raimon knew about these thoughts of hers he'd fall about laughing, or he'd tell her off for making life more complicated than it needs to be. Men don't go in for all this ruminating.

There is, however, at least one man who does. Matteo Spadaro has ruminated enough to put himself under the skin of a fearful and hurt woman. Maybe it's not Bruna who Blanca wants to get to know.... Maybe it's Matteo, the man who painted her as she is.

'Sol, have you got a photograph of Matteo Spadaro?'

Her sister promised to look. Meanwhile Blanca has done a search on the internet: Sicily + Literature. The search engine thinks for a bit and comes up on the screen with a few names: Pirandello, Giovanni Verga, Lampedusa, Leonardo Sciascia... There's a lot for an island of 25,000 square kilometres. But there's an even more impressive list, of people who made Sicily their creative base or were inspired by it in their work: Goethe, Maupassant, Wilde, Nabokov. No sign of her novelist. She does a search specifically for him: Matteo Spadaro.

No pages exclusively for him. No pictures. His name is on bestselling lists. *Scordare il dolore* third edition.

Scordare il dolore, the biggest selling novel from Sicily; *Scordare il dolore*, runaway success across Italy; *Scordare il dolore*, translated into French and English.

Matteo Spadaro? Born in Naples nearly forty years ago. This is his first novel. Nothing else.

Raimon arrives and asks 'What are you doing?'

'I've got to go to Sicily,' she answers, laughing.

'Mmmmmm... Sicily...,' says Raimon.

Blanca thinks: now he's going to say why don't we go? He'll say do you want to go? Do you want to go to Sicily?

'Mmmmmm... Bellini. *Norma.*'

He leaves the room humming the melody.

Since that day I haven't been able to focus on anything. I'd wake up and my first thought was about Massimo, or Isabella, or the two of them. The day turned into a constant struggle, and failure, to get my head to deal with other matters. If I tried to take my mind off it all, I failed time and time again: listening to music, all the words of every song seemed to be about affairs and new loves; every TV kiss made me think not about us but Massimo and Isabella.... I soon found it was easier to latch on to everyday things rather than anything transcendental. So when I felt my obsession was about to take control of me I thought about the shopping list: no plain yoghurt left, almost out of coffee and fruit.

At better moments I took refuge in the novel I was reading and it was certainly preferable to escape into wonderful words and lovely sentences rather than macaroni, biscuits and fabric softener.

Massimo was ever further away from me, following the line, I believe, of 'the less we talk, the less we fight'. Both of us were tense, bad tempered, and we barely slept. Flavia and Giulia, the poor things, said less and less by the day, and weren't laughing.

This dreadful situation lasted almost a whole month. A month on automatic pilot. I had no desire or energy to go to work but I did, and I managed to get through my classes the same way as Giulia did her vegetables. When school finished, and for the first time in my life, I wasn't dying for the moment I saw my daughters. I knew the delight of seeing them would only last five minutes and then they'd get on my nerves and it'd end up with me shouting and them crying.

47

I did of course go and collect them, and we went straight home, avoiding the centre of town and the people we knew who always stopped us and tried to engage in meaningless conversation. I wasn't thrilled at the thought of being at home either. I didn't know where to put myself and wandered from room to room doing nothing very much at all.

From time to time I tried telling myself maybe you're making the whole thing up, maybe there's nothing going on at all. But there wasn't a shred of doubt. I didn't know if Massimo was sleeping with her, but he had feelings for her, and that perhaps hurt even more.

The worst thing of all was that I couldn't see a way out. The end to this torment, uncovering the truth, would only mean the end of our marriage. I was convinced of it. Did I want that? I did want to be able to go back to a life of calm tranquillity, that I did want.

That Saturday Massimo was on duty all night. For the first time in many years I decided I wasn't going to stay at home on my own, kids asleep and the television on.

I called a babysitter and phoned Dario. We used to bump into each other occasionally, on the street or outside the cinema, but I'd never called him at all since we broke up. He had been my great love for four years, my first adult relationship, and although Massimo had never let it be known to me, I knew he didn't like the fact we were still friends. Dario was surprised, and I would say flattered, by my call, and invited me to dinner at the trattoria just down the street. It didn't cross my mind for a second what people who saw us might think, or if anyone would mention it to Massimo. I can't say if that's because my conscience was clear or because I couldn't have cared less if that had happened.

I made that phonecall on impulse, not thinking why I was doing so or what consequences it might have, but as we clinked our glasses of Chianti, I knew exactly why I had. Dario, the great seducer, looked at me with warmth, understanding and desire. I had no intention of anything more than dinner with him, but the way he looked at me, like a soothing lotion on my lacerated mind, was very welcome.

We talked about mutual friends, our jobs, and made little gentle inroads into our past history. Dario, ever the smart one, didn't ask why I'd phoned now, after such a long time. Neither did he enquire into how life was as mother to a family, nor if I was happy with Massimo. He didn't give me the slightest chance to reveal my wounds to him. It was a cleansing evening of softness and gentleness.

He walked me home just after midnight, and he kissed me ever so lightly on the lips.

I went straight to the answering machine but there weren't any calls. That was the first time I'd thought about Massimo all evening, and the feeling of lightness was so lovely... I fell asleep immediately.

The telephone woke me before dawn and as I picked up the handset I saw the red figures on the alarm clock, 5.35. My heart had time to race and beat wildly against my chest.

'Is that Massimo Allori's wife?'

'Yes.'

'Dr Allori has had an accident. I'm calling from the hospital.'

'He's had an accident at the hospital? What sort of accident do you mean?'

'No, he's had a car accident, on the Messina road.'

'How is he?'

'Serious, but not life-threatening.'

I stayed there, sitting up in bed, for some time, in the dark and with the phone in my hand.

My life had crashed at ninety miles an hour.

Chapter Three

I asked my mother to come and look after the kids. When I opened the door she hugged me and said 'My poor Bruna, my poor girl!' I was very touched by my mother, such a severe mother and never indulgent to her children, being so openly compassionate at that moment. I had little time to spare but as we hugged I was able to say, 'I'm scared.' My mother held me tight with characteristic strength, and in a firm but gentle voice said 'I know you're afraid, of course you are, but I'll be with you.'

My God! My mother consoling me without judging, without scolding! Perhaps I'd been wrong not to choose her as my confidante. Perhaps she'd have exorcised all of my demons, as she did when I was little, with dampened flannels on my forehead to lower my fever. Too late now. I rushed off to the hospital, a little less fear in my body.

When I arrived at the emergency room, my sister

Cecilia and her husband Taddeo were there waiting for me. My mother had phoned them. I was reassured to see them, but then I got a fright. The expression on their faces signalled nothing good.

'Is Massimo dead?' I asked, hugging my sister.

'No! He's not dead. They're sure he'll pull through...'

In that case... why the overwhelming look of anxiety in their eyes? Something was wrong, something was very very wrong.

'Bruna, listen...' My elder sister took my hands in hers and looked me in the eye. 'It's best I tell you now: Massimo wasn't on his own in the car. There was a girl with him and she's in hospital too. Apparently she's a doctor...'

What happened to me then was truly colossal: I finally had confirmation of the suspicions which had tortured me for months, finally I could show everyone, and especially myself, that I wasn't going crazy, and that I was right. In some way the nightmare had ended... and at the same time I was dumbstruck by surprise. My sister found this perfectly logical, of course, not knowing the story, and said to me: 'Cry, Bruna, cry...' to get me to react.

And cry I did; I howled with tears and felt the pain of betrayal as if the thought had never crossed my mind even for a moment. Did I not think I'd prepared myself to find out Massimo was cheating on me? Hadn't I pictured this scenario a thousand times?

I found myself released from Cecilia's arms and, I don't know quite how, I reached Massimo's bedside. He had one arm bandaged up and cuts on his face and neck. His pained eyes opened and he said, very softly:

'Bruna.'

'Were you with Isabella?'

'Yes.'

It was a statement of defeat, shame and cowardice.

'How long have you been together?'

'Bruna, please... I'm tired. We can talk later.'

'No. I've been wanting to talk about this for a year now. How long?'

'I don't know... about three months. But... don't you want to know how I'm feeling?'

I was incandescent with rage.

'No, Massimo, I don't want to know how you're feeling. What about you? Do you want to know how I'm feeling?

Poor poor Bruna! Blanca stops reading to take a breath. This Massimo is a complete wanker!

She ought not to be working today. Raimon has a day off and they'd thought of spending it together, going to an exhibition, or for lunch somewhere special, or to the cinema.... But her mother-in-law phoned to say she wasn't well, and seeing as Violeta is away.... She doesn't mind their plans being upset: she's been dying to know what happens next in *Forget the Pain*.

The doorbell rings. It's a delivery from the greengrocer's. Blanca rummages through the pockets of the coat hanging in the hallway, looking for a coin to tip the lad who's arrived arms laden with lettuce, spring onions, aubergines and courgettes, cooking apples, mandarins and grapes.

There's nothing there apart from a packet of mint gum. She puts her hand in the pockets of Raimon's anorak: yes! She picks out a couple of coins.

The boy's gone and she's quietly putting away the shopping. As she does, she remembers there was something else in the anorak pocket.... She goes to the door and puts her hand in the pocket. She does so with trepidation and, for no reason she can fathom, remembers the very few times in her life she's had to clean a fish before cooking it.

It's a card from some restaurant. She breathes deeply, the weight off her back. It's just a restaurant card. She smiles: what was she expecting? A card from some 'rooms to rent by the hour' joint?

She puts it back in the pocket and returns to the kitchen: tomatoes and lettuce in the drawer, mandarins and grapes in the fruit bowl...

She's gone back to the hallway without quite knowing how. She isn't sure if her brain gave her the instruction. She picks up the card: Restaurant Paradis. It all looks very sophisticated, very expensive, very romantic. She's never been there.

He must have gone with some famous musician who was passing through Barcelona.... Very odd he hadn't mentioned it...! Whenever they come across a good restaurant they note it down so they can go.... He can't have liked it much.

Her heart begins to leap up and down, and it lodges in her mouth. On the back of the card there's a telephone number written down. She immediately looks around for the cordless phone and prepares to dial. My God, what's she doing? For heaven's sake! Raimon isn't Massimo! She's not Bruna!

She has to sit down. Her legs are shaking too much. She feels short of breath. She decides to go to the bathroom and splash water on her face. She sits on the toilet and closes her eyes, trying to calm herself down, but within her there's a murmur, incessant though it makes no sound. It's Bruna's butterflies. She catches sight of herself in the mirror and is tempted to burst out laughing. Breathless, telephone in hand, dishevelled and sitting on the toilet. What a sight.

'Nothing's wrong. There must be an explanation to all this: the restaurant, the phone number... must be.' She breathes slowly and deeply. Her heart slowly returns to its normal beat. 'When Raimon gets here, I'll ask him all about it, calmly, openly, as I always have. And he'll give me all the answers.' But just thinking about it makes her feel weak: she's ashamed to admit to her suspicions and thinks Raimon will be offended, and with good reason. She would be, too.

Raimon arrives a short while later, when Blanca's got some colour back, and her breathing's under control again. The little wings have quietened down. In her head she's rehearsed twenty ways of asking the question. Eventually, in what's supposed to be a natural tone, like someone who doesn't really care too much, she comes out with:

'Where's the Restaurant Paradis?'

Raimon looks at her absently.

'The Paradis? No idea. Don't think I've ever heard of it.'

Blanca produces a little laugh. Oooh. How forced.

'I was looking for some change, in your anorak, and I found a card from the Restaurant Paradis. Have you been there?'

He doesn't seem to want to look at it too closely. But he gives away no fleeting hint of discomfort.

'Well, er... I suppose so, if I've got their card.... Don't remember though...'

He goes and puts the coffee on. As if nothing has happened. An unimportant question and a vague answer. But how can he not remember going to a top-class restaurant unless he goes there all the time? There's silence for a few minutes and then suddenly Raimon says: 'Oh, yes, I know. I went there with that Russian pianist who was over a couple of weeks ago. The conductor asked me if I'd take him to lunch...'

Blanca breathes out, but watches her husband carefully, and it seems to her as if he is breathing more deeply than she.

Massimo's left arm was in a real mess, and one of the wounds to his neck was very bad. He had a fever and his breathing was strained. The sedatives meant he was drowsy most of the time.

Isabella was all right. She only had two broken ribs due to the jerk of the seatbelt. Doctor Ferrara, Massimo's colleague, told me this; he had to call on his great professionalism to avoid embarrassment at my questioning, and give me the medical information just as if it were any other patient.

I don't know if this man knew everything or if he was as surprised as I was, because, incredible as it might seem, I was dumbfounded. Obviously I knew Massimo had been flirting with Isabella, or in the worst of cases falling in love with her.... But I'd never have imagined that he was carrying on a more or less stable relationship, deceiving me in a regular and premeditated way, lying to me when he said he was on night duty, and sleeping with her in some hotel room while I was watching television at home to combat my insomnia.

There were so many reasons for the pain that I hurt all over. Like hundreds of little knives digging into me everywhere, or burning hot oil splashing and scalding my head, as if to pierce me.... I couldn't decide what was most hurtful: the daily lying, the whole betrayal, the purely physical unfaithfulness, the possibility that he loved her, the recklessness, the total irresponsibility which meant he endangered our marriage, our family, and therefore the happiness of his daughters. What kind of man had I married? An immature hopeless nothing? A cynical liar? An idiot?

Perhaps there'd been some reason which had led Massimo to behave like this. Don't they say that if a relationship is going well it's virtually impossible for a third person to come between? I knew our marriage wasn't going through the best of times, but up to now I'd been convinced things had started to deteriorate as a result of Massimo's changing attitude. What if it had been the other way round? What if Massimo had started to drift away because our relationship had disappointed him? Was it possible that he'd ended up in Isabella's arms, driven there by my veiled criticisms, the sharpness in my nature, my obsessive demands for the perfect love?

Massimo's love had been so passionate at the beginning.... When I met him I'd only had a couple of emotional attachments. The first was an adolescent romance which was so inconsequential it barely left a trace, and the second was Dario, a tortured affair which almost wiped out forever my capacity to love. I had handed myself over so openly, so freely and so blindly to a being who was egocentric and seductively puerile. After making such a crass mistake I swore to myself I would think very carefully before falling in love again, and that's how it was for years. Until I met Massimo.

He was the young surgeon who operated on my father and he caught my eye immediately. His assurance, both firm and affectionate. His passion when it came to showing feelings. That look of a helpless child which lay hidden behind the assurance and passion.

All the same I wanted to protect myself and Massimo had to work hard to make me fall in love. He did it, as he has always done when he wants something, with dedication, persistence and enthusiasm. When finally one August night on the beach he convinced me, I believed with love's unshakeable faith that I had met the man who would make me happy. Massimo took me by the hands and said, 'Come with me, Bruna, come down to the sea,' and he took me right down to the water's edge where I could feel the chilly splashes like a summer shower starting to fall. 'Let's jump into the sea, Bruna!' said Massimo, like a little child overexcited with a new toy. 'Let's jump in! Don't be afraid! Don't you trust me?'

And then, when he'd asked that question, I took his face in both hands and asked: 'Look me in the eye.' Massimo's eyes: wide, deep, restless as oceans. There was no calm, there was nothing to offer me safety. There was a chance of a storm, but even so I said yes, because there also was light and water, all I needed to live.

When we came out of the sea, Massimo picked up a handful of sand and offered it to me. There were little white pebbles and a shell. I took it. I still have it. It's white and yellow, with little ridges, perfect.

Far away from the waves, nothing has spoilt its pattern, which has survived longer than our love.

Raimon never made any emotional and emphatic declarations of love. He won Blanca's love gently, quietly, daily. With conversation, music, looks and silences. Discreetly and deeply. Then one evening he asked her to go with him to a concert of chamber music. They were sitting together in the audience, Blanca was watching at him out of the corner of her eye, and he saw that little look in her gaze, that expression of incomparable tenderness. She took his hand and Raimon squeezed it tight. They looked at each other and she said, silently, just with the movement of her lips, I love you, and his eyes filled with tears.

And Blanca, every time she recalls the moment, also gets tearful.

This afternoon she just can't get down to work, but neither is she in the mood to spend it with Raimon. She improvises a headache, a need to get some air, and a quick call to Anna. 'I'm going round the sales, see if I can't clear my head,' and Raimon says goodbye with a concerned glance.

When she's sitting opposite Anna, at the table in the chocolate shop, two sweet steaming cups between them, she can't help the confession which, like a waterfall, gushes from her. She shares her worries with her friend, concentrating on the discovery of the card, and not letting on that she's been obsessing for days.

Anna listens dutifully and laughs when Blanca says that to begin with Raimon didn't remember the name of the restaurant. She says, with aggressive casualness, 'Typical... saying he doesn't remember anything so he can play for time and come up with a story. I do the same thing myself when my husband peppers me with questions...'

Blanca recalls Raimon's initial casual reaction: 'Paradis? No, don't think I've ever heard of it.' and then a moment or two later the apparently logical explanation: 'Oh, yes, I went there with that Russian pianist...' Could he possibly have made it up? No, okay, maybe Anna does that. But not Raimon, no way.

When Cecilia and Taddeo went off to work, my mother arrived at the hospital after dropping the kids off at school. She'd told them their father had hurt his arm, and they wanted to go and see him after school. I told her to come and have some breakfast with me in the hospital cafeteria. I hadn't prepared anything at all so I simply hit her with it:

'Massimo wasn't alone in the car. In fact he lied to me about being on duty last night. He's got a lover.'

Hearing myself say those words was like someone spitting in my face. My husband had a lover. Massimo had a lover. A lover. This wasn't fiction, this wasn't a film. It was happening to me.

I burnt my tongue on the coffee and I knew this scene was in fact reality. My mother was stunned. She said nothing, but momentarily I read reproach in her look. I can't say what she was reproaching me for – haven't you been there for him? Have you been going around looking a mess when he comes home? Haven't you been affectionate?

I got up without giving her a chance to reply. I spent the entire day at the hospital, in the little smokers' room, wondering whether or not to go and see Isabella. I was dying to, and had no desire to. I wanted to see her eye to eye, and the thought of catching sight of her terrified me. I felt the need to talk to her and I dreaded hearing her voice. My sister Paola, who came to see me in the afternoon, convinced me:

'I can understand that you want to give her a hard time, but it would be bad for you too.... You've got enough to deal with as it is.'

And what would I say to her anyway? Tell her off for falling in love? For not thinking about me and my kids? It was Massimo who should have thought about it! For the time being I made do with imagining Isabella anxiously waiting for the door to open and me appearing.

Over the days that Massimo was in hospital I began my 'round of chats'. I spoke to my sisters, to my brother Guido who'd come from Paris with his girlfriend Oriana to see me; I wasn't that close to her, but I trusted her. Oriana was a sensible woman, and above all she'd been through a separation. I wanted to know every opinion, evaluate every point of view; I wanted to have all the information I could and not jump to a hasty decision.

More than anything I thought about my daughters. Flavia was five years old. Giulia just three.

How could I allow this calamity into their lives? How could I permit them to suffer, so young? How could I let their father's absence at home cause them continual pain? If Massimo wasn't responsible enough to protect them from himself, then it would have to be me.

When I stopped thinking about the girls for a short while and thought about myself, things changed significantly. What did I want? Did I want to live with a man who didn't have respect for me?

Did I want Massimo by my side at any price? Was I able to forgive the lies and forget all about it?

My 'advisory council' surprised me. I'd expected 50% in favour of separation and 50% for reconciliation. I'd sensed that my sisters would lean towards keeping the family together... but Guido? Oriana, who'd separated herself just the year before? ALL of them, all four, told me they thought I should try and rebuild my marriage. The reasoning they employed most was not about the children; most of the time what I heard them saying, in dozens of different ways, was: you and Massimo love each other.

Could this really be? Could Massimo love me in spite of all this? Aren't loving someone and deliberately hurting them mutually exclusive? Perhaps not. Perhaps Massimo was going through a personal crisis that had nothing to do with me, and had felt some urge to break all the rules. Perhaps Isabella was no more than the means, the vehicle, the excuse. I wanted desperately to be able to dignify it all.

'Our relationship will never be the same again, never,' I said.

'You're right, it won't, it'll be different, but not necessarily worse,' said Paola, or Cecilia, or Guido, or Oriana. And whichever of them added, 'Everyone has the right to make a mistake, Bruna.'

My brother played a significant role in the 'advisory council': he brought to bear the male point of view. He said things which I instantly rejected, but later made me think over and over again, and eventually were helpful to me. 'When a man goes after other women, it's got nothing to do with love or respect for the woman he loves. It's a basic instinct. Basically, it can be repressed or not, but we've all got it.' All? I pictured my brothers-in-law, my male friends, the headmaster at school, the men I didn't know but admired.... All of them?

Massimo seemed a little less evil, a little less cynical, a little more human.

When I said that the deception hurt more than the actual infidelity, and recalled the packs of everyday, premeditated deliberate lies, Guido stopped me, and with a lot of common sense he said, 'The only lie to be borne in mind is the first one. After that, once into the spiral of deceit, you've no choice but to keep going right to the end.'

And so the days went by. Massimo was getting much better, and I heard Isabella had left the hospital. Having her a long way away, not sharing the same building as us, was for me an incomprehensibly simple relief. Since the day of the accident we hadn't mentioned her by name. In actual fact, all we said to each other was to do with the kids or his medical condition.

Doctor Ferrara informed me that if we wanted, Massimo could continue his recuperation at home. Deep down, I didn't want this, because I knew that it would force me into making a decision. The most difficult decision of my entire life.

Knowing Massimo, I was sure he too had set the deadline at his coming home. He wanted to let his feelings cool off in order to be able to appeal to my sense of responsibility and good judgement, of that I was sure. I wasn't expecting spectacular acts of repentance or attempts at cheap seduction. He knew me, and was aware that for the moment he could only convince me through reason. Emotionally, the wounds were too great.

The day we returned home, Flavia and Giulia were waiting for us with my mother, all dressed up and their hair neatly brushed, with a huge sign which read: WELCOME HOME DADDY.

I looked at the banner, and then my mother, thanking

her for the gesture with my eyes. Always the same, my mother: now cold, now warm.

Massimo kissed the girls and broke into a smile for the first time since the accident. Within me, like a flashgun going off, I felt a little rush of expectation that we would be happy again.

That afternoon, Cecilia and Taddeo took the girls off to the cinema, 'so you can be on you own'. Massimo sat up on the bed with lots of cushions behind his back. He'd shaved, and looked almost healthy. I sat at the foot of the bed and took a deep breath.

'Tell me, Bruna.'

Wow. We're not off to a good start. Tell me? Shouldn't you be the one saying how sorry I am, I still love you, I don't know how it happened?

'We need to talk, don't we, Massimo?'

He sighs. He looks at me, saying with his eyes 'if there's no alternative'. I think he's about to say do you want to separate?, or maybe what do you want us to do?, or perhaps I'd like to try and save our love for each other.

I've got my answer more or less prepared. I feel terribly hurt; it'll take time to recover, but I want to try. I want to save our marriage and our family because I think, in spite of everything, that it's worth the effort. Mind you, only if he is able to convince me that he loves me and that Isabella was a mistake, a dreadful mistake that we will both forget together.

But Massimo says nothing like what I'd thought he would. Massimo, very very gravely, says:

'I'm sorry, Bruna, but I think we should separate.'

Is this his way of saying sorry? Getting in first, in case it's what I want?

'Maybe not, Massimo,' I say gently, in a voice I don't recognise.

Massimo closes his eyes momentarily. I'd say he's plucking up courage.

'Bruna. I'm in love with Isabella. I'm sorry. I never thought this would happen to me. I thought our love would last for ever. But I think it's best for everyone if you and I separate.'

'Best for who? Best for you and for Isabella, obviously. Not for the girls, nor for me.'

I couldn't stop the words coming out of my mouth. The silence is dense, thick, and it stops me from thinking clearly. I force myself.

'Listen, Massimo... don't you think that might be a very hasty decision.... Maybe we both ought to work at it and try and... maybe...'

'Bruna,' Massimo interrupts me, saying my name with a tenderness I don't remember. 'Bruna, don't make this even more difficult. The decision has been made.'

I can feel the flames rising into my cheeks. My whole being is a blazing firebrand.

'No, Massimo! You're wrong! What do you mean "the decision has been made"? It's our marriage. It's our family. It's our future. That means the decision has to be ours and we haven't made it yet!'

I leave the room, slamming the door. Propped up against the corridor wall, I put my hand on my chest to try and slow down my heartbeat.

Forgive? How do you forgive betrayal? Out of generosity? Blanca suspects that in cases like Bruna's there's as much generosity as selfishness. Or fear. Fear of ending up alone. Wanting to hold on to the man you love.

God, if that's what love is.... being resigned, forgiving, conforming. These are words which transport her to the world of nuns. She believes love should be free and demanding. If the couple in the novel try and carry on, Massimo won't be free and Bruna's demands will fade into non-existence.

Would she forgive? No. Even if she really put her mind to it, Blanca knows she wouldn't be able to get over an infidelity. She and Raimon have talked about it. For both of them, being faithful is one of the fundamentals of love. Loyalty, sincerity, compromise. No. She wouldn't forgive.

Maybe it's because she hasn't got children to cope with. Maybe it's because she still feels young and brave. Perhaps because she wants to maintain her dignity, or that she's too proud. Dignity and pride are too similar. It's difficult to tell one from the other.

She mulls this over for a while and comes to the conclusion that it's not so much about her dignity as his. Could she continue to love a man she didn't think was honest and worthy? How would she look Raimon in the eye if he'd betrayed her?

All of a sudden, she misses Raimon madly.

She turns the computer off. She gets dressed and goes out. She doesn't know where to go. Where does this nagging stem from? Butterflies are dancing around in her stomach. What's that distant, nasty voice deep inside her saying? She can't make it out. It's telling her something's not right, that she should go and find out what it is.

She gets into the car and goes off to the Restaurant Paradis. The address has engraved itself effortlessly in her mind. She stops outside, double parked. Now what? Is she going to spend all day here waiting to see Raimon go in with a woman? What makes her think he'd be stupid enough to go back to the same restaurant now she's found the card?

Suddenly she manages to picture herself from the outside. Shut in the car, watching, like a detective on a TV show. An ironical little smile emerges on her face. Right: tonight she'll tell Raimon all about it and they'll piss themselves laughing. The little voice dies away, slowly. The dancing wings gradually stop fluttering.

After the conversation I went out of the house without saying goodbye. All I had with me was a packet of cigarettes, a lighter and my keys. I walked quickly and with my head down, desperately hoping not to bump into anyone I knew. I felt inexplicably ashamed.

I avoided the busiest streets, but when I got near to the Greek Theatre I heard someone calling out 'Bruna! Bruna!' I didn't look up. I kept walking, almost running, as if they were chasing me. As if they might tell me off for something I'd done wrong!

I stopped for breath when I got to the steps which lead down to Mazzaro. At that time of day there weren't many people around and I felt a little safer. I went down the steps slowly and the sea breeze brought me scents of cool freshness. I stopped and looked around silently. Spring had arrived while I had been suffering.

While my world had been reduced to the hospital, the nights of tears in a bed too wide, the doubts, the fighting with my pride, and giving in to misery, the bougainvillaeas had flowered and the world was fuchsia, violet, orange and scarlet. And down there, the blue of the sea.

I didn't go down to the beach. Part way I sat down on the steps to quietly watch the sea and Isola Bella. The island floated miraculously in the midst of the blue. Like me.

I breathed. It was hard to believe but... Massimo had left me and I was alive. The incredulity kept me still for a long while. But I'd decided which would be my next port of call.

As I retraced my steps back towards the centre of town, my heart was beating more normally and the butterflies' dance in my stomach was more gentle.

I headed towards Villa Comunale, the prettiest gardens in Taormina, to see how spring had set in there. It did so every year. And this year it would too.

Villa Comunale is on the top of a cliff and I arrived puffing and a bit sweaty. But the gift awaiting me there was worth it.

The fruit trees had started to blossom, some quite shamelessly. Peaches, plums, cherries covered in pink flower, white, bathed in light, almost transparent. There were lovetrees overflowing with magenta blossom. And silver birches and acacias.

Lobelia filled corners with blue, alongside white and bright yellow camomile. Hyacinths of every colour under the sun were growing on a bank: violet, pale yellow, mauve.

Before my eyes, the sea. And over there, far away, the silhouette of Etna. The volcano which never sleeps.

What must go on in there, in the guts of Etna, to make it spit out fire and smoke? I felt sure the insides of *the volcano were no more churned up than my own. The butterflies were getting more and more agitated and I felt short of breath.*

'Living next to a volcano makes you more alert,' my grandmother used to say. I hadn't been alert enough. I hadn't taken enough care of my love and now I'd been left without it. Living without love.

I lean forward and throw up. Like Etna. I want to spit out the butterflies, open my mouth so they escape in a frantic flapping of wings; rid myself of torment.

Mount Etna. The biggest active volcano in Europe. Most of the time the lava comes out of secondary vents. Eruptions of the main crater are much less frequent, but it's not unusual to see it smoking.

The volcano's outflow has turned the Lower Valley into a fertile land where almond trees, olives, vines, orange and lemon trees grow, greenness which contrasts with the black of the Bove Valley, where rivers of lava have flown for centuries.

Even more contrast: in winter, Mount Etna's summit is covered in snow, and the cold white picture can be stained by hot red vomit from deep inside.

The guidebooks highlight another volcano which is still active: Stromboli. Blanca is devouring information about Sicily. Stromboli! The island where Bergman and Rossellini fell in love...! She reads that you can take a boat trip out to watch the spectacle of burning lava flow down to the sea.

Oh my God. It's been a long time since Blanca's wanted to do something so much. She wants to see Sicily. Mount Etna. Stromboli. Taormina. She closes her eyes and arches her back. She's going to tell Raimon that this summer she wants to go to

Sicily. Why's she never been there before? She'll call Sol and ask her about the trip she made there with Jaume, years ago.

Spadaro's novel is obviously good. Who wouldn't be able to produce a wonderful story with such an extraordinary backdrop? The metaphors write themselves. Bruna loves and hates Massimo the same as Sicily loves and fears Etna, the all-powerful mountain which rules and destroys.

Chapter Four

On the way back from Villa Comunale to home – barely a quarter of an hour – the colours, smells, the freshness of the air all drifted away from me. When I put the key in the lock I was once again the subdued, dark Bruna who'd left our bedroom just hours ago. Why was I coming back? What was I supposed to do that night? Sleep in the double bed with Massimo as if nothing had happened? Go and sleep on the sofa, me, so as to avoid contact with him? Throw the convalescent Massimo who'd just had an accident out of the house?

I suppose what I should have done is get in the car and drive a long way away from Taormina. Open the window and get the wind on my face, press down on the accelerator and scream. What my body needed was all of that, and then to spend the night in some hotel on the road where nobody could find me. Disappear.

But... what about the kids? Their father couldn't look after them. What's more, if I wasn't there by bedtime, Flavia would be scared and little Giulia would cry.

But when I got inside, Massimo wasn't there. For once, he'd finally done something right. The desolate silence in the flat suddenly overpowered me and I cried for a long time, until I heard children's voices in the hallway outside; I hurriedly washed my face and went to greet my daughters.

Cecilia gave me a look full of concern and murmured, 'Do you want me to stay for supper?' I didn't even reply but very definitely the thought of cooking and giving the girls their supper presented itself as an insurmountable challenge. I didn't feel I had it in me at all. As well as that I could sense a rage building inside me that made me fear an uncontrollable outburst and the last thing I wanted was to make Flavia and Giulia pay for it all. In the end I asked my sister to stay. My daughters looked at me with both unease and surprise. I knew why: it was the first time in their lives they'd seen me abdicate my responsibilities as a mother.

It was a dreadful night. Long and horrible. Any thought, however brief or fleeting, caused me a rush of pain. I just wanted not to think and this, which has always been difficult for me, was at that time absolutely impossible.

If I cast my mind way back, I'd find a glorious past I'd lost for ever – all the years that Massimo and I had shared in love with each other – or if I remembered the year just gone I'd only find pain, months of anguish, and then it was hard to resist the temptation to go back over each and every one of the lies, day by day. That evening I had felt so awful and I'd phoned him to ask him to come home early and he said he had an emergency operation...

could he have been with her? Was Massimo such a bad, heartless person? His flat denials, looking so offended, after the Palermo conference: 'Of course I haven't been doing anything with Isabella!' My pathetic attempts to get to the heart of the fear: 'Shall we invite your colleagues from the hospital round for dinner? Tell Isabella as well...' If Massimo was a cruel unscrupulous man... then what was I? Hopelessly ingenuous? A submissive desperate woman? Had I been abandoned by the intelligence which had got me through life, turning me into a being which couldn't even defend itself from its nearest enemy?

If I tried to look to the future, I felt overrun by panic and could only see myself on the edge of a terrifying abyss or staring into a tunnel of pure blackness.

I was transfixed by the past and the future, prevented from moving a millimetre from that instant of pain and anguish. There was nothing, nor anybody, that could enter my thoughts and console me, not even – and this is saying something – my daughters, because the thought of them going through such a trauma as a divorce was horrific. I saw my life as a succession of errors and wrong moves. I'd made mistakes in the most important questions in my life: choosing the man with whom to share it, joining a profession which had become boring, and having two children I couldn't see myself being able to raise in a happy environment. I hadn't even managed to gather round me true friends who could be by my side through this mess.

The house and the town where I lived had ceased to feel welcoming, and I wasn't young enough to start all over again and not old enough to let people just look after *me. What's more, above all, first and foremost, despite everything, I loved Massimo and missed him, and would have given anything to be able to take refuge in his arms that night.*

But instead of that, when I closed my eyes I saw his lips running over an unknown skin, his voice murmuring gentle words in another woman's ear, his expert surgeon's hands exploring a body which was not mine.

The pain was so searing I had to open my eyes and breathe deeply two or three times. There was nothing that could soothe the rawness of my soul.

Blanca, curled up safe in Raimon's arms, that night tells him everything she's found out about Sicily and its volcanoes. She suggests going there in the summer, but doesn't mention the pathetic sight of her in the car keeping watch on a restaurant. They don't piss themselves laughing. That night she doesn't see anything amusing in any of that.

Raimon makes love to her delicately and passionately, as always. With the same delicacy and passion as when he releases the purest of notes from his violin.

The next day, Sunday, she wakes to the steady gaze of Raimon's eyes. He kisses her immediately.

'Were you thinking how gorgeous I am?' she asks jokingly.

'No. I was thinking how much I love you,' he says more seriously.

He tells her he's going out to get the paper and some fresh croissants. Blanca stays in bed, savouring the pleasure of a weekend morning. From the bed she observes the chunk of sky she can see through the window and the uppermost branches of the acacias in the street. Not a single cloud interrupts the blue. But then the wicked little voice starts to interrupt the calm of the Sunday morning.

Unable to restrain herself – like an alcoholic looking at a bottle of Scotch or a compulsive gambler with a fruit machine – she gathers herself up to look at her husband's bedside table. She opens the drawer and rummages around, not knowing what she's looking for.

Blanca sighs and falls back again onto the mattress. The window, the sky, the acacias. Like a maggot, the little voice starts gnawing at her. As if in a comic book, with a good angel and a mischievous demon at either shoulder, both whispering into her ear.

She can only hear the little demon. Does she really want to invade her husband's privacy? Is she actually doing this? She thinks it's contemptible, deceitful, intolerable... but the little voice doesn't give up, and for the first time in her life she believes in the famous female intuition.

She breathes, breathes again. Everything's all right. Nothing's the matter. She hears the key in the lock and quickly closes the drawer. Raimon calls out from the kitchen, 'Blanca my honeybunch, breakfast's ready!'

As they have breakfast, sitting opposite each other with Raimon flicking through the newspaper and her pretending to be looking at the colour supplement, Blanca comes to the conclusion it's time to get things sorted out. No more of this rubbish. The problem is the amount of time she spends at home on her own. If she had a job which meant she had to get out of the house and interact with people then she wouldn't have her head stuffed full of surreal suspicion. Spadaro's novel was the last straw! But she can't even consider dropping it half way through, and she can't abandon Bruna.

She'll finish translating *Forget the Pain* and look for another job, even if it's part time. She can't let her paranoia harm her relationship with Raimon. Raimon is not like Massimo, she tells herself again. And she? Is she like Bruna?

The next day while I was having a cup of coffee I noticed the little light on the answering machine flashing. There were affectionate messages from my mother, my sisters, Oriana and Dario. I felt a little less denigrated, but only a little. I couldn't rid myself of the conviction that because I'd been unable to hold on to the heart of the man I loved, I was worthless.

What did Isabella have that I didn't? For a start she was younger. Probably more easygoing and fun. She was attractive, sure of herself, and most probably was full of unwavering admiration for Massimo.

I'd been very demanding with him. I am demanding. I wanted a perfect husband, a perfect life, and was always wanting more. To always set the bar very high, never take your eye off the ball, maintain the romance, make our love into something quite unique.... Perhaps, though, I didn't give enough. But deep down I refused to believe it. I sincerely thought I had always been extremely generous with him. I didn't deserve this treatment. But obviously Massimo hadn't sat down and weighed up whether I deserved it or not before he cheated on me.

This last thought made me listen to the messages on the machine again. Before, I hadn't paid it much attention, I'd just thought... 'Bruna, I hear things aren't going well with Massimo. You know how it is, Taormina's a small place.... Has the time come to make good that promise you made me?' It was the ironic and affectionate voice of Dario. I couldn't stop myself smiling, although sadly. When Dario and I had decided to break up, seeing as we hadn't fought and were so fond of each other, I told him, 'You've got to promise that we'll stay friends.' And he said, 'Okay, but you've got to promise that when you're married you'll have a bit on the side with me.' This little episode had never crossed my mind again, but it had Dario's... apparently. I knew it wasn't a serious proposition, but it made me think: would I have been able to be unfaithful to Massimo? Could it have happened to me, falling in love with someone else? I honestly thought it would have been very difficult, but not impossible. But it would have been another thing for that love to outweigh my sense of commitment and responsibility. All this had just been thrown up in the air.

At lunchtime I phoned Massimo. I wanted to know how and when we were going to tell the children. My legs felt they were about to give way any second, and I propped myself against the wall. It had to be done though. I could read the questioning in the eyes of the elder one: are you sure you haven't tried hard enough? In the little one's eyes, bright and wide as an open window, all I could see was incredulity. Was it really Massimo and I inflicting all this suffering on our own daughters. The same two people who had cared for them, loved them, protected them ever since the day they came into the world? We were sitting beside each other on the sofa, but I didn't feel he was by my side, nor anywhere near me.

Massimo had asked his sister to come at six and take the girls out, to take their minds off the difficult time they'd been through. Daniella arrived on time, just as we were finishing our talk. She gave me an affectionate hug but didn't say anything. When she and the girls went out of the door, Massimo sat down in the nearest chair and put his head in his hands. He was crying. I'd never seen him cry. And I couldn't help it, I went and put my hand on his head. He looked at me with all the desolation in the world.

'I didn't want to hurt you all.'

I was very grateful to him for that sentence.... Finally I could again believe he was telling the truth.

He packed two suitcases with clothes and shoes, and collected up some papers from the study. I stayed sitting in the chair where he'd cried, unable to react. The tears were trickling down my face and neck and made me feel all right. I was crying softly, gently, finally. I was very very sad, but the anger was slowly dying down.

Then Massimo came out of the bedroom with the suitcases. I stood up, my arms by my sides.

'Will you just wipe away those tears,' he then said. 'I won't let you make me feel guilty. I haven't killed anyone.'

I rubbed the palms of my hands over my cheeks until it hurt. My Massimo, the one who'd been crying in that same room a few minutes before, had gone again.

'Go,' I said.

And he did. He left me without a kiss, a hug, a handshake. Without a word of affection, without a loving look. He left behind twelve years of his life, of mine, of ours, all the life we'd built together, and pulled the door closed. I stayed still where I was, for how long I don't know. I felt the slam of the door like a slap in the face. I knew his attitude was only being defensive. Massimo felt *as guilty as if he had actually killed someone. But I wasn't about to be understanding with the immature child who'd just gone out of the door. He was a man and he'd acted despicably.*

Slowly I started to be able to move again. I went to the cabinet in the dining room and poured myself a martini. Maybe the last mistake in my long list had been to cry over that love.

Defying her principles and trampling on her own ethics, Blanca acquires the habit of snooping through her husband's things. It's an offloading of adrenaline that both fires her up and relaxes her at the same time. Pockets, wallet, drawers, files. She never finds anything odd.

She wouldn't be able to explain what drives her to do these things. She's not looking for anything in particular. She just has this suspicion that she'll find... what? She doesn't know.

However much she has this feeling he's hiding some secret, she finds it very hard to believe he could be having a bit on the side. A bit on the side. Cheating on someone. Horrible expressions when they're about you.

She hears the key in the lock. My God, her heart's going to stop. It's slowing down already... it's going to stop. Now it's going faster and faster.

'Helloooo!' the familiar beloved voice.

When Raimon sits down next to her and puts his hand on her thigh, Blanca looks at him out of the corner of her eye. How stupid she is, thinking this man with the boyish profile has been deceiving her. He turns and looks at her with a smile.

'What's up with you?'

How can she have thought that behind those honey-coloured

eyes lay hidden an awful secret? Could Raimon hug her, as he's doing now, if he'd just been with another woman? He's not a cynic. Not Raimon.

While Raimon's watching the news, Blanca sits herself up.

'I'm tired. I'm going to head off to bed.'

In other words she is capable of lying, so why not him?

She's not tired. She's agitated and unsettled. Raimon comes quietly into the room and gets into bed. He hugs her from behind. That familiar warmth. Everything's all right.

And everything is all right for a couple of days. She gets back to Spadaro's novel. Back to her dictionaries, the story of Bruna and Massimo, of beautiful Taormina. She works hard, and well. As she does so, efficiently, concentrating, a thought burrows its way into her: why don't I just come out and ask him, openly? Why don't I do what I've always done, trust him, look to him for reassurance? Because she'd have to admit to her failings? She'll do it. She doesn't want this mist hanging over their heads for ever. Their relationship is clear, transparent, and must continue to be so.

She'll call him and ask him to come home early. No special dinners or romantic trappings. Like two adults, sincere adults, sitting opposite each other, she'll say to him, looking him straight in the eye, 'Raimon, for a few days I've been getting anxious because of that Italian novel I'm translating. It's all about a marriage breaking up because of someone else. And I've got it into my head that it could happen to us.'

And Raimon will say (he does say): 'No, it won't happen to us, we love each other too much.'

Blanca will carry on: 'But the couple in the novel loved each other too.... All marriages run the risk!'

Raimon will answer firmly (he does answer firmly): 'Not us.

80

I can't fall in love with anyone if I'm already in love with you.'

And she, Blanca, with a big smile, almost a laugh, will say, 'Perhaps not fall in love... but the flesh is weak.'

Raimon will smile too and say... But Raimon doesn't smile, doesn't say anything. There's a very uncomfortable silence.

'Raimon?!'

'Yes?'

'What's wrong?'

'I don't want to talk about this any more. It's putting me in a bad mood and it's pointless.'

Blanca takes a step forward and falls, falls down and down, fast, into an endless chasm. For her it's a clear confession. Without saying so, Raimon has admitted the subject of infidelity makes him uncomfortable. And there can only be one reason. He feels guilty.

'Is there something you want to tell me?'

Raimon, looking grim and losing his patience, gets up and mutters a few words under his breath which Blanca can't quite hear, and leaves the room. A few minutes later she hears the sound of the violin and it sounds to her like a lament.

Before he goes to bed Raimon goes to give her a kiss. Come to bed with me, he says seductively. Blanca can't stop herself from waving him away. She can't bear the thought of physical contact, and even less a suggestive proposition.

She can see how the warning lights have come on in Raimon's eyes. She knows his eyes. A few words, but icy ones: 'I don't know what's going on with you, but it's got nothing to do with me. When you feel we can get back to normal, let me know.'

And to Blanca's disbelief, her man scrupulously observes this plan. Starting the very next morning he starts ignoring her and acting offended, while the anger gradually wells up in her. With every day that goes by she is more and more convinced that Raimon's attitude confirms his guilt. It's true she has no proof he's being unfaithful, but she has no intention of debasing herself by asking him straight out again. No more hysterical searches through pockets. Bruna was so right: sometimes there is behaviour which says much more than evidence.

Chapter Five

Over the next few days, I searched desperately and unceasingly for thoughts which might bring me some relief. The most effective was 'better this than an illness'.

To put it another way, in the great scheme of tragedy and suffering that is shared out between every human being and through which every family must go at some stage or other, I would rather Massimo's loveless betrayal than for one of the girls, or indeed he himself, to become seriously ill. And while my lust for life wasn't exactly at its strongest I was prepared to admit that separation – the collapse of the family such as we'd known it – was better than my getting ill. The children needed me.

At the same time I should acknowledge that the thought of Massimo worrying about me and looking after me was tempting...

But there were moments when even this idea wasn't

enough to relieve my anguish; when I felt that illness, pain, even death itself wouldn't have harmed our bond and that if we loved each other we would have been able to cope with any of these things.

When the man you love stops loving you and falls for another woman it brings about a sense of powerlessness which I can only compare to the death of a loved one. It gives you a nagging ache which you can't relieve in any way. There's nothing you can do to try and alleviate the pain. I could dress Massimo's wounds, make sure he slept, give him whatever medicines he needed.... But I couldn't do anything at all to change his feelings. I looked at old photos of Massimo and studied how he looked, to see what had changed. Those eyes which had looked at me with love and desire for so long; did they now look at me without a care? Perhaps with boredom?

His voice, which had murmured such tenderness and said my name in so many different intonations, was it the same voice which coldly – almost metallically – was now telling me that he was in love with Isabella?

He'd remember when we started being together, when he kept on saying he loved me more than I did him. It was a veiled accusation. He was convinced I was still a little bit in love with Dario. I'd argue with him: 'How can you measure love? On what basis can you say you're more in love than I am? How do you measure that?' And he'd quote Saint Augustine – a leftover from his religious schooling: 'The measure of love is to love without measure.' Then he'd laugh, with a hint of sadness. 'Let it go, it's nothing. There's always one who loves more than the other. I don't mind being on the heavier side of the scales... we'll make it balance.'

Now the scales were overturned and for ever. I had to come to terms with reality: Massimo had stopped loving me, was in love with Isabella, and didn't want to live with me any more. In the future he and I would be alive, breathing, feeling things, but not sharing. It was hard to take in.

Chapter Six

Her mother and sister, for very different reasons, both think she's nuts. Her mother reckons that if she's absolutely sure Raimon has been unfaithful then there's nothing more to be said. As there are no children involved she shouldn't see him ever again, if that's what she wants. You're still young, you've got your whole life in front of you etc.

Sol simply can't believe her sister is considering dumping a relationship that had been going so well just because of some little suspicion. Blanca hasn't got any proof! It's just her being paranoid, got to be, and.... But on top of that, even if it turned out he actually was being unfaithful, she says, that wouldn't be enough to justify separating from someone you love and who loves you; that's what Sol thinks. There's the years together, the friendship, respect, the sharing, all the plans for the future... a whole load of things which can be weighed up against the pain – and it happens, no doubt about it – caused by deception.

'Anyone can make a mistake,' says Sol. 'The same sort of thing could've happened to you too, and that wouldn't have meant you didn't love Raimon.'

But... all this getting worked up, taking decisions without knowing for certain that he is in fact being unfaithful? 'But my intuition tells me.' Sol then goes up the wall. 'Intuition!? So now it's all about intuition, is it? What's going on here is that you've turned into an obsessive neurotic! I wish to God it'd never occurred to me to give you that damned Italian novel!'

Raimon doesn't go overboard protesting his innocence. He keeps silent as usual, with a hurt look about him which Sol understands – 'What do you expect?' – and Blanca hates – 'If I was truly important to him he'd be fighting tooth and nail to prove I'm wrong!' Her sister blazes 'How do you prove something doesn't exist?!' In the end, Sol gives up: if Blanca is so sure, there must be something behind it all. Maybe her relationship with Raimon is failing, albeit not exactly for the reason she suspects. Perhaps she needs to get away, go off somewhere for a while and get her thoughts straight. Work out whether she wants to spend the rest of her life with Raimon. Work out if she wants children. Work out what she wants to be when she grows up. Go away, she tells her. Go wherever you want and don't come back till you've sorted yourself out.

When she tells Raimon she wants to go off and discover Sicily, she can see the fear in his eyes. Fear of losing her for real.

'Don't go. If you want... I'll leave the orchestra, I'll look for another job that's got nothing to do with music.

Blanca looks at him in disbelief.

'What are you talking about? Give up music? Why would you do that?'

'So I can dedicate myself to you more.'

Her eyes well up. Raimon thinks she's jealous of his music and is prepared to give it up. To give up his passion.

'You couldn't live without music.'

'Yes I could. Yes I can. What I can't do is live without you.'

So... okay. She's now prepared to accept that Raimon does love her. And? She still loves him. And? Their relationship can never go back to how it was before, pure and solid. Their love has been tainted by suspicion, like a ripe fruit that's been bruised and will end up going rotten. Best to let it go now.

Does she have an obligation to fight to save it? She didn't cause the damage.

Who can make her eat a fruit that doesn't appeal to her? Can she cut out the affected area and carry on munching away as if nothing's happened? Maybe somebody can, maybe her sister's tough enough, but she can't. She hasn't got the stomach for it.

She moves in with Sol. Furious. Sad. Raimon calls her, comes to see her, looks at her with those defenceless eyes of his. And she just sees him betraying her, lying to her, deceiving her.

She asks him to bring round the novel she's been translating and the disk. She wants to get it finished, she hasn't got much left.

Her return into Bruna's world relieves the pain a little.

Infidelity is again fiction, the broken marriage is Bruna's and Massimo's, not hers. Taormina instead of Barcelona. Only when she's working does her stomach not churn.

She gets up early, doesn't look in any mirrors and has a black coffee. She sits down at the computer.

A few days later, Massimo told me he'd applied for a transfer to the hospital in Palermo, and that it was very likely he'd get it. 'We want to leave Taormina,' he said. I did a quick calculation of the positives and negatives this would mean to me. The kids would have to travel to the capital every fortnight but it would save me having to let them go to their place during the week. At the same time I suddenly wouldn't have to worry about bumping into Massimo or Isabella, together or separately, anywhere around town. On balance it was clearly positive so I just said 'All right, you'll let me know then.'

And it all happened. He got the transfer and the two of them went off to live in Palermo. Like a pair of newly-weds in a small cosy flat, probably. No responsibilities, no baggage, like a young lad, just as he wanted. Best of luck to him.

It didn't hurt to imagine him in this new role because the actor playing it wasn't anything like my Massimo. My companion of more than a decade had literally vanished into thin air; he didn't exist any more.

Inevitably, however, the first weekend Flavia and Giulia had to spend with their father came around. I packed a bag with clothes, pyjamas, toothbrushes. As if they were going off on a school camping trip.

Massimo came to collect them right on time and when I looked out of the window I saw he'd been thoughtful enough to come on his own. A little kiss for each of them and a 'Be good'. Bye bye. See you on Sunday.

It was six o'clock on a Friday afternoon. I had a whole weekend to myself. I could do whatever I wanted with it. As if I'd want to spend it all sleeping! How many times had I wished for a couple of hours just for me in the last few years...

Now, sitting on the double bed, in the empty house, I didn't know what to do with so many hours. There was nothing I felt like doing: not reading, or going to see a film, phoning someone.

I went out to get away from the emptiness and the silence, but I couldn't handle the noise in the streets of the centre of town.

I ended up at the gardens of the Villa Comunale. Sitting beside some blue lilies and with the blue sea before me, I watched how the evening fell on Mount Etna, as dusk arrived in Taormina.

I took a deep breath and the air filled me with an unfamiliar tranquillity. The beauty was so sad.... What was I doing there all on my own on a Friday night? Where was my life, pinned on people and feelings I'd thought were unmovable? Had a girl who didn't know me at all and probably never wished me any harm blown through my life like a tornado and taken everything away? I couldn't allow myself the ingenuity to believe it. How easy it could have been: like the little children who bundle up their fears in an incarnation of evil, the devil, the witch, the bogeyman, Isabella.

It's clear the pillars holding me up were unstable. The wind had got up for sure, but the structure hadn't been up to it. Something had gone wrong. Was it all down to Massimo? Or had I also failed?

The reality is that I was alone that evening, watching the Sicilian sea, and not knowing where to start to rebuild my crumbled life. What pillars must I choose, how should I go about it to make sure it doesn't all collapse again?

The therapy of pain: 'It'll go away, it will go away.'

The only consolation you can give to someone suffering extreme pain. And my pain was extreme, I swear. A mixture of all the pains: loneliness, fear, jealousy, longing, rage, sadness. A concentration of pain in the centre of my chest which I knew must cave in at some time or another. Suddenly I realised there was no fluttering of butterflies. There was just the pain, hard as a stone.

I stayed there for some time. The night fell, the silhouette of the volcano disappeared and the crickets started up. It had been very difficult for me to admit that with the passing of time happiness consists, basically, of the absence of pain. I took it as the price you pay for being an adult.

Now, with my fortieth birthday just over the horizon, I understood, and planned to take on, that my only objective from now on was to forget the pain. Forget the pain in order to survive.

That's the sentence with which Matteo Spadaro ends the novel. Afterwards there's the epilogue which she read on the very first day before she started translating. Those questions which, as she now realises, had shaken the columns on which her very self was built.

What should I do? Acknowledge the pain, look it in the eye and learn to live with it? Or the very opposite: run away from thoughts of martyrdom and force myself to ignore the pain?

There's still time: she can still call Raimon and tell him 'I lost my senses for a few days, I'm very sorry,' and run home and pretend nothing's happened and everything's just as wonderful as before. But that's not what her body demands. She wants everything to explode, put it all to the test, send it all flying and see what's left. That's what she wants.

Blanca decides she's going to Sicily. She wants to see Mount Etna. She wants to see Taormina and Isola Bella, and the gardens of Villa Comunale. She wants to go to Stromboli and see the rivers of lava pour into the sea. She wants to survive in order to forget the pain.

Part II

Chapter Seven

'Blanca Dausà?'

'Yes.'

'Seat 17B. Boarding gate 32 at 11.50.'

'Thank you.'

Before the plane took off, I buried myself in the guide to Sicily I'd bought the day before. I just wanted to be there. I didn't want to think about going away, leaving Barcelona behind, flying away.

Three seas bathe the coast of Sicily, as its ancient name 'Trinacria', the three-cornered island, suggests. At different times in its history, it has been ruled over by the Greeks, the Romans, Byzantines, Arabs, Normans and Spain, and each of these cultures has left its mark on the island...

I had to stop over at Naples and get on a flight to Catania, the city in thrall of Mount Etna. I'd just read that across its history, Catania had suffered frequent earthquakes and floods of lava, and that in 1693 it was completely destroyed by a fit of temper from the volcano. But the Catanians, far from falling out of love with the mountain, went back and rebuilt the city at the foot of the volcano and reconstructed the buildings with volcanic rock and lava.

Men and women with an obstinate determination to survive. It was just what I needed.

As I came out of the terminal wheeling my luggage behind me, looking around for a taxi, Etna greeted me cordially. I stood still before it in wonder, watching the column of smoke, slim and well defined, that emerged from the mouth of the volcano. It was a welcome by smoke signals, like the Red Indians in the old American movies.

The taxi left me at the door of an inexpensive cosy-looking little hotel I'd found in the guidebook. It was just off a big square, in the very heart of Catania.

The days began, inevitably, with a descent into hell. Just as I awoke, as my brain started to function, the first thought I had was always the same: Raimon's infidelity and our separation. But once I'd managed to get myself up and out, there were so many things to see in Sicily that the days weren't long enough. Driving around the roads on the island in a hire car, no one knowing exactly where I was, I managed to feel, if not quite happy, at least free of worry. That in itself was quite something. As Bruna would say, I managed to stop the dancing butterflies in my stomach. The tranquillity was a fiction, I wasn't kidding myself, but I preferred to achieve it by driving around Sicily rather than with Tranquilium, Valium or any other *ium*.

I made a phone call every day to Barcelona, one day to my

mother, the next to Sol, but I never asked after Raimon, and they followed my instructions by not mentioning him.

Only ignorance could afford me a relative calm.

The first Sunday came around. I'd woken early and had been battling through the good old days for some time, stretched out on the bed in that hotel room, looking up at the sadness of the yellowing ceiling. I got up reluctantly and showered and dressed, and unenthusiastically went down to breakfast. Signora Leoni brought it to me with her usual generous smile and regulation *'Buon giorno, Blanca!'* and explained that on Sunday mornings in Piazza Carlo Alberto there was an antiques market. I was still in luck.

The hours passed slowly but pleasantly among the cruet sets and glass salt cellars, gilded rococo mirrors, modernist brooches, little porcelain jars and above all pieces of Sicilian ceramic: cups, plates, masks and tiles, all greens and blues.

During the week I'd been almost every day to the fish and vegetable market near the Duomo. I was looking for noise, and colour, and movement, and people; I'd found the right place. The Sicilians babbled incessantly and at high speed, all gesticulation, with a shriek in their voice and an infectious vitality.

With my senses stimulated by the surroundings, memories were banished and the pain gave way to the smells – mandarins, coffee, dark chocolate, and colours – olive oil, red wine, honey, the feel – the skin of the peaches, the smooth cold of ceramic, the tastes – marzipan layered with lemon, little balls of ricotta cheese in batter, fresh pasta cooked a million ways, and the sounds – the human hubbub, the whistles from the espresso machines, the horns of the fishing boats coming into harbour.

With the pain deadened and memory drugged, I started to

think about my immediate future. Had I gone to Sicily just for a holiday, to enjoy myself, to get away? Or had I gone with some hidden aim which was starting to reveal itself shyly? Shyly, or clearly?

Bruna had been with me on my journey since the first day. I felt her so close to me I was sometimes tempted to talk to her. And if I couldn't turn her into a flesh and blood Sicilian woman, why couldn't I go and meet her creator? I felt a burning curiosity to find out how this man, this novice writer, had been able to get inside the emotions of a woman tormented by betrayal. The male brain which had described with such precision the mind of a wounded female.

The mind of the fictional Bruna, the mind of the real-life Blanca.

Why not?

My sister didn't seem surprised when I asked her for the address and phone number of the Sicilian publishers of *Scordare il dolore*. They were based in Palermo.

I thought it was more likely they'd give me Matteo Spadaro's address if I went to ask for it in person. At the same time it meant I'd be able to see Palermo, one of the towns on the island with most Catalan heritage.

With my recently acquired obsession for markets – how come some people in turmoil seek solitude and silence? – I rushed to the Vucciria, in the centre of Palermo. I'd read about the name: Vucciria... from *bocceria*, meaning market. Like the Boqueria market in Barcelona. Once I arrived there among the vegetable stalls and the shrieks of the Sicilian women I was overwhelmed by an attack of yearning. Amid the aubergines and courgettes, the olives and salt cod, the almonds and toasted hazelnuts... *mezzo chilo di pomodori maturi... può darmi un sacchetto? ... avete pesce fresco? ... vorrei due etti di prosciutto...* I cried and cried. Perhaps because I would never again go to the Boqueria with Raimon at Christmas time to buy a special lobster, he wouldn't again buy me flowers on the Ramblas, and because those wide-eyed children I'd imagined would never be born, we wouldn't share the horror of our bodies getting ancient, nor look for an old farmhouse to restore up in the hills of the Vall d'en Bas.

There, in the Vucciria, I got out my phone and called him. When he answered saying my name, 'Blanca!', I was crying so much I couldn't say a word. He repeated 'Blanca! What's wrong? Can you hear me? Blanca!' And I hung up. What could I possibly say to him? That I was convinced, and without any proof, that he had gambled with years and years of happiness to give satisfaction to his body or his mind, and ultimately his ego. My mobile rang and it was Sol, who said no she wasn't Raimon and I'd binned my future in exchange for keeping my pride. I hung up. It rang again and it was Raimon: 'Come home, come home, come home!' and I hung up. Another ring, and it was a girl from the publishers who said that Mr Spadaro would be pleased to meet me. And this last call was real.

I turned and looked around me. Laid out in rows there were gorgeous peaches, plums, pears and clementines. On the other side of the aisle the beautiful happy array of green and red peppers, bulbs of garlic and spring onions. I was still crying.

A fat neat-looking lady, her hair tied back in a ponytail, came over to me. *'Coso posso fare per lei?'* She was a real *Mamma* and I felt I could rest my head on her colossal bosom, but instead of that I started running and rushed out of the market.

Matteo Spadaro lived at number 12 Via Cavour. According to the map of Palermo I had in my bag, it wasn't very far. I just had to go up Via Roma and after the Museum of Archaeology I'd come to the street. On the way there I stopped at a coffee shop and had a hot cappuccino. I also took the opportunity to try and sort my appearance back to normal after all the tears at the Vucciria.

I was nervous. I didn't know what my pretext was for going to meet the writer. Perhaps I didn't need a pretext and it was perfectly logical that after translating *Scordare il dolore* and being on holiday in Sicily I should drop in to say hello to the author.

But I knew this wasn't just a normal courtesy call. I wasn't going as a translator but as a reader. I didn't want to get to know the writer of a bestseller all over Europe... I just wanted to ask him about Bruna, the character with whom I'd identified to such an inconceivable extent.

What if Spadaro was one of those very aloof writers, or very shy, or behaved like some genius irritated by someone interrupting his creative processes? No. The publishers had told me that Mr Spadaro 'would be delighted to receive me in his home'.

And what would he look like? Had I imagined him in any particular way? Yes, I imagined him with dark curly hair and very dark eyes. Bronzed skin and three days' beard on him. Like all Sicilians I suppose.

Via Cavour. Number 12. A single storey house with a front door painted bright green and wooden shutters on the windows. Outside, a small cast-iron letterbox with the words 'Matteo Spadaro, Psychiatrist'.

'Psychiatrist'? I turned away without ringing and started walking round the block of little houses. This detail filled in a few gaps.... So Spadaro had another profession... that's why he started writing late on and didn't get his first novel published until his forties. And obviously it was easy to believe how his understanding of feminine psychology helped create the character of Bruna.

I finally gathered enough courage to ring the bell. He opened the door himself, or at least I assumed it was him because he looked the typical Sicilian and said in a deep voice 'Blanca?'

He welcomed me with wonderful island warmth: openness, sweet wine, and chocolate.

He talked and talked and talked, with lots of gesture and hand waving. He wanted to know everything about the translation, about Barcelona, and me. We immediately hit it off. Matteo Spadaro was just how I'd hoped he'd be. No. He was better than I'd hoped.

As if it could've turned out any different, my unbridled enthusiasm for Sicily went down well with him. We went through the places I shouldn't miss: churches, beauty spots, restaurants, open-air markets…. The island seemed even more enticing when he offered it, as if he was putting before me a dish of pasta he'd made with his own hands. I interrupted him with a knowing smile: 'I want to go to Taormina as well….' Matteo took only a few seconds to say: 'Yes, of course… beautiful Taormina. Shame about the tourist invasion.' I dared to say 'It's you who's made me want to go there,' and he said 'When you write, you always tend to idealise a bit. Maybe you'll be disappointed…'

We exchanged telephone numbers and we said goodbye on the doorstep, he shaking my hand effusively and promising to call me when he was in Barcelona. He closed the door gently after giving me a look of affection. I hadn't asked him anything about Bruna or how he'd been able to read with such precision the thoughts of a woman betrayed. I hadn't told him that his novel had affected me deeply and had destroyed my marriage. I hadn't admitted to him that I'd come to Sicily to get away from the grief. There'd be time for that. My infallable female intuition – what if it wasn't infallible? What if I was wrong about Raimon? – was telling me I'd see Matteo Spadaro again soon enough.

My phone rang about an hour later. I was in the middle of eating spaghetti al pesto at a little inn on Piazza Marina.

'Are you going back to Catania today?'

'Yes, of course.'

'You can't. You must stay. You have to see the Vucciria at night. You're at the Marina Inn, you say? They've got rooms. Ask them if you can stay there tonight.

They had a room free and I felt like staying and going to the Vucciria with Matteo Spadaro. And because I wanted to do it, I did it. The long lost sense of not having to explain anything to anyone made me feel hopelessly young.

Before we went to the market, Matteo took me to the Museo delle Marionette. When we came back out again, Matteo murmured 'Perfect.'

'What's perfect?' I asked.

'It's dark now. The Vucciria will be lit up by now.'

The lighting at the market consisted of dozens of ordinary bulbs strung over the stalls and protected by red canopies. The effect was one to fall in love with. Matteo led me through the aisles, often stopping to talk to the stallholders and admiring the colour of the turnips or the scent of the strawberries. It was all smells and all movement.

'Now we're going to have the best sardines in Palermo.'

It was a very strange night. I couldn't help seeing myself

from the outside. What was I doing sitting here with a man I'd met that very same afternoon, in a bar in the old town of Palermo, eating battered sardines? We talked about Lampedusa and his book *Gattopardo*, about Stromboli and the volcanoes of the Garrotxa back in Catalonia, about the mafia and Gaudí, and the Sicilian separatist movement and Catalan nationalism.

Later we went on round the other markets in Palermo like a Way of the Cross, and ended up at what they call the Borgo Vecchio, very near the port. 'It stays open all night,' he said, as if it were a promise.

But it had started to drizzle and Matteo gently took my elbow and showed me back to the little hotel. He asked me if I was thinking of staying in Sicily for a while. I answered that I didn't know, and that I didn't have any fixed plans. 'I'll call you,' he said.

He left me at the door and I watched him go off in the rain, his hands in his pockets and his back hunched over.

When I got into bed the sheets seemed a little damp to me and I felt a desperate need to be in my own bed, at home, in Barcelona, with Raimon by my side. I missed him dreadfully, but every time I thought of him I saw his lips approaching a woman I didn't know but had imagined with a thousand different faces. What must it be like to kiss different lips? I hadn't done it since the day I met Raimon. Why did I imagine him only kissing her, not making love? Was my imagination unable to go beyond a certain frontier of pain? Or was it that a kiss better represented infidelity and betrayal?

A kiss, the most intimate way of saying I love you, I desire you, I want to be very close to you. And Raimon had kissed lips which were not mine. I coiled myself up with my hands on my belly, the pain so intense I was scared. I cried and cried until I fell asleep.

The next day I went back to Catania. The journey helped me to think over what I should do. My mother and Sol were asking me to explain my plans... but I didn't have any plans. For all my going round in circles, there was nothing to make me go home. A little nest of fury had formed within me. Raimon hadn't stopped me from leaving Barcelona. Either he didn't love me enough or he was feeling guilty. In any event I didn't feel I had the strength to attempt a reconciliation and so I knew that if I went back to Barcelona our separation would become permanent.

Those days in Sicily were like an intermission, a period in limbo, as if I were suspended in mid air or floating in amniotic fluid: no obligations, no decisions, almost no pain.

And so I gave myself another week's extension. Matteo called me the next day. 'Would you like me to take you to Stromboli?' My heart started to waltz and my enthusiastic reply was a bit embarrassing. I wanted to see the island with the volcano which never sleeps, the place where Bergman and Rossellini fell in love, and I wanted to go with Spadaro.

That's how one April day I left Catania with my mind full of open wounds, hurtful images behind my eyes, a fistful of tears in my stomach, a deep deep sadness within me... and I arrived in Milazzo in north-east Sicily, travelling light, having lost along the way the wounds, the hurtful images, the fistful of tears and the sadness.

Matteo had come to pick me up in his car and the journey was a gentle tumble into happiness. It was a bright clear morning and all my eyes saw was beauty. Matteo drove in silence, beside me, and I could feel my spirit opening itself out, all doors and windows wide open.

'I'm sure there isn't a place on earth of more special beauty than the Aeolian Islands. It's all smoke and water. We'll be able to see all of them from Capo Milazzo: little mounds of still smouldering ashes.'

Matteo stopped talking just as this vision appeared before us: the Aeolians surrounded by blue, Calabria in the distance. We got out of the car and the stiff breeze blew through my hair and my thoughts. My eyes began to fill up, and this time crying was a respite, a relief. The beauty was so overwhelming it left no room for anything else.

Matteo came up to me. 'Are you all right?' Without looking at him, not knowing how near he was, not caring if anyone else could hear me, I told him how I was convinced Raimon had been unfaithful to me, and about the unbearable pain and the closeness I felt to Bruna, the reasons I'd run away to Sicily.

Matteo took my hand and led me towards the car. 'Let's go to Stromboli.'

I think that if he'd said let's go and dive into the sea I'd have followed him there too.

We caught the ferry to Lipari, the main island in the Aeolians, Matteo telling me all about how the island is full of hot springs and geysers, 'like you were in a *bain-marie*. From there we'll get a boat to Vulcano and Stromboli. There won't be time for anything else. We'll go to Vulcano first, because it's best to sail into Stromboli in the early evening: as night falls the sight of the lava flowing down into the sea is at its most impressive.'

Amid the fire, water, smoke, sand, lava and mud, time went by. Sweet, gentle, silent. The world – pain, decisions – had stopped, and the expression in Matteo's eyes was ever warmer.

The Aeolian Islands bombard the senses constantly: the white cliffs and black rivers of Lipari; the smell of sulphur on Vulcano and the unrepeatable experience, different every evening, of Stromboli.

Our return to Catania in the pitch black night was accompanied by the voice of Lucio Dalla: *Te voglio bene assai, ma tanto tanto bene sai.* We didn't say a word the entire journey. When we got to Palermo, Matteo invited me to a coffee at his house, but before he put the machine on, in the hallway, he took me gently by the elbows.

When Matteo put his hands to my face and drew nearer, very very slowly, to my lips, I had enough time to think that I hadn't been thinking about my husband (just as Raimon hadn't thought about me when he was kissing her).

Chapter Eight

'It's absurd for you to be in Catania, in a hotel, when you could be staying at my house in Palermo.'

Matteo said it without a blink, as if it were the most natural thing in the world. And I, incredible as it might seem, also thought it logical. I nodded in agreement and he added 'You can stay as many days as you like.'

With that sentence he'd just made it easy. We weren't taking any earth-shattering steps, there were no long-term, or short-term, future plans, no commitments of any kind. He was a friend who was having me to stay at his house for a while. That's all. Well, there was sex too, obviously. But nothing else.

At the age of thirty, I discovered that I too could feel good having sex with someone for whom I felt nothing deeper than kind understanding. I also felt the sweet taste of revenge. I hadn't set out to 'do it back to him' but I knew that in any other circumstances I wouldn't have ended up in Matteo's bed.

I too could desire him while still loving Raimon at the same time. I too could do both.

'You're staying at Matteo Spadaro's house?' Sol was stunned.

'Don't you think that's okay?'

'I don't think it's okay or not. I think it's surprising. But you're a big girl now...'

'Don't tell Raimon.'

'That's the first thing I was thinking of doing...'

'Listen, I can do whatever I want. He has!'

'Blanca, dear lovely Blanca, don't start looking for pathetic excuses, because no one's asking you to justify anything...'

'You don't agree with me, do you?'

'About what?'

'About me deciding to separate.'

'My opinion is completely unimportant. I don't even know what it is. All I do know is that if I had the chance to have Jaume here with me I wouldn't reject him because of an error. But don't take any notice of me, I don't see things the same way as everybody else...'

I recalled my sister in the days and weeks following Jaume's death. The opaque look she had in her eyes and the permanently cracked voice. And my mother saying:

'You'll see, my child ... you will get through all this. And one day, maybe, in the future...'

Sol, with the last grain of energy she had, said:

'I can't think about the future. If I thought I'd never see him again, I wouldn't be able to get up in the morning. The only way I'm able to start the day is by thinking "I won't see him today. I've got to get through the day as best I can but I won't see him." And then I think maybe tomorrow... or the next day...'

I didn't want to, but I found myself wondering whether I'd 'rather' Raimon had died. I realised it was a dreadful thought to have, but in a way it was as if for me the Raimon I loved *had* died. If he were no longer there I'd be able to remember him with my love intact and respect his memory, perhaps even to the point of myth. But as it was, now, I couldn't even miss him. Who would I be missing? The man who'd deceived me? The man who'd betrayed my confidence? The man who'd been able to do it once and so could do it again?

I know perfectly well what my sister would have said if I'd confessed these thoughts to her: there's nothing worse than death. Death is absolute, irreversible; it's nothingness. The grief it causes is futile, total.

And my grief, what was that like? As each day went by it was a confirmation of Raimon's guilt. The pain was lacerating, intense, and continual. But there were little coping strategies to combat it. I was able to imagine the day would come when I wouldn't care Raimon had been unfaithful to me. And we would be together again. Not Sol. Her grief was hard as a stone and nothing could crush it.

Other people's experiences, however, don't configure our feelings. Above all I felt hurt, and all I wanted was to find something to reduce the pain of my wounds. Matteo was the best balsam.

He made me laugh, and made me believe I was good to be with.

Palermo was a friendly city and with Matteo spending so much time at the hospital, I felt comfortable at his house and nothing was tempting me to go back.

Precisely because of that, seeing my return as a distant possibility, I decided to write a letter to Raimon. I was well aware I couldn't stay in Sicily for weeks without saying a word to him. When I left, I'd asked him not to call me, to let me be on my own, for as long as I needed, and I'd promised that when I got back we'd talk.

He had respected my wishes – it goes without saying that, privately, I wished he hadn't – and I felt bad about keeping him completely in the dark for any longer. I still couldn't clear up the uncertainty for him because I was still submerged in it...

I went – not without some emotion – into Matteo's study. It was a small room, full of light, furnished in clean lines which combined the lightness of birchwood and aluminium. The bare white walls and the wooden floor, a yellow so pale it looked white, inspired a feeling of serenity.

I sat down, reverently, at the computer: it was probably in this very room, sitting in this very chair, that Matteo had written *Scordare il dolore*. One day he must have opened a new document when Bruna didn't exist and when he saved it a while later she had been born. Creativity was a mystery, to me. A mystery which I respected and admired. The same thing happened with Raimon, when he shut himself away in the little music room and made up a melody out of nothing. First one note, then another. First one word, then another.

I also opened a new document and I wrote:

Dear Raimon,

I don't want any more time to go by without writing to you. I know you must be concerned. Well, I suppose you are, anyway. I don't know anything for sure now. The earth began to shake under my feet a few weeks ago and I still haven't been able to find peace for a moment. I would like to be able to tell you that I have made a decision and tell you why, but that is not how it is. I am still spending all my time licking my wounds and really, not wishing to hide anything from you, I am not making much progress.

I feel hurt, and when I miss you – because I miss you a lot – I remember that you are the one who has caused me pain.

I am sure there are many people who think I am exaggerating. But you and I know I am not. I am sure that if you suspected I had been unfaihful to you then you would feel the same as I do now. I don't feel I have it in me to go back to where we were as if nothing had happened. There are just two possibilities: either I am right and you have meddled with and sullied our love, or I am wrong, a possessive neurotic who could spoil your life. Neither option is pleasant, is it? I would like to be generous, or brave, or unfeeling, and believe you without going round in circles any more. I am sorry, I cannot. I cannot ignore what my heart tells me. And it has not escaped me that your love for me could not go on intact if I have offended you by abandoning my confidence in you without reason. You know how it is: my idea of love is very old-fashioned, or very naïve.

Part of me hates you for not defending with sufficient determination what we had. The foundations on which I had built my way of being have been shaken because I am not sure if yours are the same. We were a common construction and now, now I know that the foundations of my construction could be shaken again, in the future, many times, and also when I least expect it. Living with such uncertainty is making me very uneasy and I estimate that it will take a long time for me to get back to feeling at peace. It is a little like living at the foot of Mount Etna, knowing it could explode at any moment.

Maybe I am wrong and you have acted properly, defending an offence to your dignity ahead of our love. Maybe you did not need to demonstrate your innocence, or maybe your not being innocent is not that serious. I am not certain that my way of understanding love is the best. But it is difficult for me to give it up. It was built up over the years, through the way I was brought up and certain beliefs. I felt comfortable with it and now it has disappeared.

I will still stay in Sicily for a while, depleting my savings, and trying to find out if I need to start loving in a different way, or instead find a man who knows how, and wants, to love as I ask him to. I cannot be more sincere.

When I get home I will let you know. I can feel sure that music will keep you company. See you soon.

Blanca

I sent the e-mail and was about to turn the computer off when I saw a document of Matteo's entitled *The Cat*. I opened it without thinking.

Il suo nome è Laura... Her name is Laura. She can be cruel and vulnerable. She's disturbing.

She arrived out of the blue from another country across the Mediterranean. She recklessly displayed her wounds and demanded closeness with an untrue lightness, as if she didn't need it to survive but desired it

feverishly. Like a cat which has just squandered one of its
lives falling off a roof; licking its wounds, half helpless,
half proud.

He, Ivo, a man used to hiding his old scars and
protecting himself from future injury, stowed away in a
safe place his good sense, and offered himself with
generosity to the cruel, vulnerable, disturbing girl.

As had happened with *Forget the Pain*, the opening words
sparked my curiosity almost like a shove in the back. Also,
Matteo hadn't mentioned a second novel to me. I was violating
his privacy, but it didn't seem to me that there could be
anything wrong with it. I recalled the sensation of anguish
which I felt the first time I rummaged through Raimon's coat
pockets. But there, as with other things, it's all about starting.
As with infidelity: the first time a fall into an abyss, the second
a collapse in a heap, the rest little stumbles.

I went back to Matteo's story.

Laura had just lost her innocence. The love of her life had
bared his teeth. The prince had turned back into a frog
and the princess had run off to Sicily to find out if all men
ended up being toads.

They met at the Vucciria market, among the stalls of
salted cod, the strong smell of octopus frying at the fish
bars, and the bright colours of the fruitsellers' stands.
Laura looked around anxiously, wanting to bottle the
smells, frame the colours and record the sounds. The man,
Ivo, despite all his principles, the rules he'd laid down for
himself so firmly years before, invited her to a dinner of
sardines in Palermo.

The Vucciria? Palermo sardines? I couldn't help but smile. From the look of it, our brief but intense friendship had clearly inspired Matteo to write. He'd understand me.

Laura showed she was ready for the game of seduction. Ivo realised, however, that the desire he saw in her eyes was the desire of revenge. And so that evening he said goodnight with just a peck on the cheek, but the flavour of her skin was exciting. He walked away in the rain, knowing she was watching him.

Good Lord! How did Matteo know I stayed there in the doorway watching him go off into the distance in the rain? Did that first innocent kiss really excite him? Oh, please... what was I doing identifying Ivo with Matteo, confusing life with literature to that extent?

For Matteo to get inspiration from reality, as all writers do from time to time, is one thing, but for him to be recounting blow by blow our story, his own feelings... that was very much another.

No, it's okay: Matteo was not Ivo, and I was not Laura. He'd simply taken us as starting points from where to draw the characters. That's all.

Ivo and Laura shared a real passion for Sicily. He a blessed son of the island, she a dazzled outsider. Above all, they sought out visual pleasure. Both were fired by the pure beauty of the landscape.

Laura wanted to go to Stromboli and the volcanic islands. She explained how in her country there were volcanoes too, but much less aggressive than the Sicilian

ones. Peaceful sleeping volcanoes which were there with
you but never called out to you.

Oh... oh! This Laura really was very like her, too much so!
Good thing he changed her name...

Ivo drove to Milazzo without speaking. He sensed Laura
beside him, awestruck at the scenery, and didn't want to
distract her. He could see her increasingly captivated,
concentrating on every stretch of the island which flashed
by her. The music of Franco Batiatto, the singer from
Catania, played on the radio.

At Capo Milazzo they got out of the car and were
confronted by an almost aggressive beauty, the Aeolian
Islands smoking out of blue.

Her gaze still on the emerging smoke, Laura started
telling Ivo about her musician husband, how he'd been
unfaithful, and how she felt betrayed; and of her escape to
Sicily. It was the living image of pain.

When they got back into the car, Lucio Dalla's
'Caruso' playing, Ivo stroked the hand Laura had left
resting on the seat. 'I want you very much', Ivo said, and
Laura said it back to him.

I'd gone bright red, and wasn't sure whether it was through
embarrassment or indignation. I mean, hadn't Matteo gone a
bit far? This was my story, my desperation, these were my
tears! How could he dare transcribe it all line by line in a novel
without even asking me?

I did my best to calm down. Maybe he was just using a few
real-life details and then the novel would go off on various

paths.... Perhaps he planned to write it first and then ask my permission to publish it.... And maybe, maybe Matteo Spadaro was a greedy opportunist.

The text ended there, so I needed to be patient. Matteo didn't know I'd found the novel, so he'd freely carry on writing. Yes, I wanted to wait and see to what extent he'd continue to steal my life to create Laura's.

That evening, when Matteo came home, I made yet another discovery which alerted my curiosity. On the shelf in the hallway, Matteo left his keys and the letters he'd brought in from the postbox outside. On top of the pile was a pink envelope which I noticed. 'Dottore Matteo Spadaro. 12, Via Cavour, Palermo.' It was clearly a child's handwriting. I turned the envelope over but the sender had only put the initials 'E.S.'

What child could be exchanging letters with Matteo? Maybe it was one of his patients with some kind of psychological difficulty who wrote in this kind of lettering...

Whatever it was I didn't dare ask Matteo. That evening a little and supposedly inoffensive secret had come between us, casting a fluttering shadow over our relationship which until now had been as clear as shallow waters.

Matteo continued to be affectionate, asking me how I was and repeating how concerned he was that one day I might go away.

I went on in limbo, in my sack of amniotic fluid. No decisions, no thinking, almost no feeling pain. I was in no hurry to return to the real world.

Chapter Nine

Ivo and Laura became aware, almost without their seeking it, of the birth of an incandescent passion between the two of them which every night set alight again the glowing embers.

I wouldn't have put it like that.... An incandescent passion? It sounded good, but.... It seemed to me that Matteo and I simply got on well with each other and, from time to time, also demonstrated our affection in a sexual way. I'd been burned enough with my anguish on leaving Barcelona. Now all I wanted was calm, friendship, and a bit of fun.

Ivo acted as part tour guide, part Pygmalion, part lover. Laura wanted to learn, to discover, to savour the beauty of Sicily.

So it's Pygmalion is it? Well I never! Just because he was ten years older than me he thought... or was it because he was a psychiatrist? Or because he'd written a successful novel? Yes, all of that was true, but it was also true that to find the subject matter for a second novel he'd had to wait to hear my sad story.

I read a whole chapter in which Matteo entertained himself describing in glorious detail Ivo and Laura's romantic encounters, the smouldering looks, the nocturnal caresses. Those two were a lot more in love than Matteo and I were. I began to doubt whether it was a literal transcription of our relationship. Maybe, in actual fact, Matteo had only used a few details so as to sketch the female character, and from then on Laura would take on her own existence and she would no longer be like me, nor would the same things happen to her.

That's when a rather Machiavellian idea occurred to me.

I left the house shortly after he did. I went to the Vucciria and bought sardines that smelled of the sea, pine nuts, cinnamon, grapes, raisins and anchovies. As I stuffed the sardines, in Matteo's kitchen, I felt like launching into 'O Sole Mio'.

He came home when it was getting dark, and I told him I'd got a surprise ready for him. He shut himself away in his study and with a smile on his face he left me to get on.

I laid the table with the everyday blue napkins, because in Matteo's house there wasn't anything unnecessary. No fancy tablecloths, no posh glasses, no candles to decorate the table.

I called him, he sat down with an amused look on his face, and I came out of the kitchen with the dish in my hands, solemnly intoning 'Sarde a Beccafico, a l'estilo Blanca'.

The dinner was very enjoyable. Matteo said it was the best stuffed sardines he'd ever had and I thanked him for his hospitality, his friendship, and for bringing all of Sicily within my reach.

I don't remember how I guided the conversation so as to end up talking about my sister Sol, as planned. Matteo looked ready and willing to listen to me. I had settled down on the sofa and wrapped myself up in the white furry rug, and Matteo was looking at me, seated in a low wide armchair, brown leather, a glass of malt whisky in his hands.

I, deliberately, began to talk about Sol, knowing that I would eventually tell him about that freezing black night, a story I had never since recounted out loud. But it was necessary, and I did it. I talked about how Sol and I sat through the long cold hours in the mountain refuge, holding each other's hands. I could still remember, with extraordinary precision, the increasing intensity of the contact as our fingers intertwined, how the sensitivity of touch grew to the point of pain, when that exhausted voice told us they had found Jaume's body.

Matteo listened in silence, occasionally proffering a look of understanding or tenderness, exquisitely attentive. I believe he understood that Sol is my sister, and that I share with her the collective memory borne out of games and secrets which only exists between siblings, but that she is also a little bit my mother, performing as she has the roles of protector and adviser ever since I've had the use of reason; and she's my friend too when suddenly the six-year age difference which makes us mother-and-daughter vanishes and we are so close we are one; and she's my workmate, when we chat for hours about books and literature, ever since she offered me a profession which allows me to be me, and free; and sometimes, very few times, she has also been my little sister, when I've been able to alleviate the huge sadness from which she is never completely free.

When I am in the dark, she offers me light. When fear freezes my blood, she gifts me warmth.

Matteo listened to me, and then he made love to me.

I only had to wait three days. One night he was up late working, and the following day I broke into his novel like a burglar and found Sol's life.

The fire in the grate splashed red reflections and warm sounds around the room. Ivo was listening. Laura was talking about her elder sister Rosanna, to whom she was devoted. A brave, sensitive woman, whom Ivo imagined dark-eyed and with a bright smile.

Rosanna was six years older than Laura and because both had lost their father when they were little, the elder sister's protective instinct had grown and they had become ever closer since. Before her eighteenth birthday, Rosanna fell in love with the brother of one of her schoolfriends. Alessandro. He was a slim boy, shy, affectionate and honest.

For Laura it was a perfect love story. They looked great together, and you could see at first sight they were made for each other. They had many things in common but were able to keep their own identities with ease. Their different personalities led them sometimes to hold irreconcilable opinions to the point of conflicting extremes, but Laura had never, ever, seen them lose respect for each other.

Rosanna and Alessandro joined forces to convince her mother and his parents that they weren't making a mistake by getting married immediately. They were only twenty but it was obvious to everyone that they had the necessary commitment to do so and for it all to work out well.

On their wedding day, Rosanna confided to her sister 'At last I feel everything is all right.' It was as if she had been twenty years waiting for this, as if she had been born with this day in mind.

The adolescent Laura engraved this declaration of love in her memory and there and then promised herself she would never get married unless she could make a similar statement.

Rosanna and Alessandro had a daughter, Grazia, and then a boy called Ruggiero. They found time for everything: they worked, they cared for the kids, they saw friends and family, and still Alessandro was able to go off up to the mountains from time to time. 'If he doesn't go every three or four weeks, he suffocates, he really does,' said Rosanna, with a smile.

He'd leave on Sunday morning at dawn, with his friends from the climbing centre, and come back late in the evening, tired, replenished with oxygen, and happy.

That winter, the children had caught every bug around, and Rosanna and Alessandro hadn't gone out for weeks, except for trips to the doctor's or the hospital. On the Saturday, both children had got up without a temperature, no cough, no upset tummies. 'Can you believe it?' Rosanna said to Laura on the phone next day. 'They're all right! Are you going to come for lunch? Alessandro's going to be out all day up in the mountains.' Laura sounded surprised. 'Is he going climbing? On the radio they said the weather was going to be very bad...'

Rosanna was very understanding. Alessandro needed to breathe. And they were always exaggerating on the radio, and he always went fully prepared. If he ever thought things were getting difficult he'd come straight down.

The two sisters had lunch with the children and spent

the afternoon watching a Bogart and Bacall film on television. A quiet Sunday afternoon like Sunday afternoons are. No foreboding, not a hint of tragedy. Absolute normality. Laura helped Rosanna with the kids' bath and supper, and once the children were in bed she went home.

When the phone rang she was in her pyjamas, reading on the sofa. Her mother was already asleep.

Her sister's voice was unbroken. There was just the slightest tremolo at the end of each word. 'He's not back yet. What do I do?'

Their mother stayed with the children and they went where the police had told them to. There they met the parents of Giorgio, the friend Alessandro had left with that morning. The lady was crying uncontrollably, and her husband was a little irritated but trying to calm her down. 'Come on, nothing's happened yet.' Laura remembers this man and his 'yet' makes her feel sick again, just as it did that night.

They were taken up to a well-equipped mountain refuge, given blankets and coffee and told to wait. Laura sat down facing her sister, on a simple wooden stool, and took her hands. Hours went by like this, in silence, looking at each other, holding hands.

As day began to return and the refuge was filled by grey light, Laura saw the aged face of her sister. The bags under her eyes, her distorted features, her fevered look. She was only twenty-five, but there was none of the carefree young Rosanna of twenty-four hours before. Getting married and being a mother twice hadn't made her older, but fear had suddenly aged her.

The door of the refuge opened, and exhausted

mountain rescue and police entered. That is when Laura
noticed the tightening squeeze of her hands. Time stopped,
and the next thirty seconds, until one of the men came
over to them, were left suspended in the air over their
heads. Rosanna looked at her and gave her a sad smile.
Laura knew that when the pause ended, when her sister
stopped looking at her, everything would change.
Rosanna's smile was that of a child who tries a cartwheel
and doesn't quite manage, or shoots for goal and misses,
or goes over the outline when she's colouring in a picture
of a horse. It turned out badly, but I did my best.

How could life turn out badly for her sister? The
rescue worker gently put his hand on her shoulder before
telling her they'd found him.

He'd done it again. All he'd changed were the names, and he'd
stolen the whole story. He'd written down, in prettier words,
everything I'd told him that night by the fireside. Sol's tragedy,
and the most dreadful night of my life, were now extracts from
a novel. What kind of writer was this Matteo Spadaro, what
kind of man? How should I react to the theft of my feelings?

For a while, my scruples disappeared like sugar dissolving in
hot coffee. I started opening the drawers of Matteo's desk and
rummaged through; suddenly, amid all the jumble of papers, I
saw the pink envelope with his name on and written in a
child's hand. The letter which had been arousing my curiosity
over the last few days. And the envelope was open. Unafraid, I
unfolded the letter.

Caro Papà: Auguri! Non ci posso credere: quaranta anni!
Anche il mio amico Andrea compie gli anni oggi (undici).

Caro papà? Matteo had a son? I skipped through the letter to the end.

Arrivederci papà! A presto!

Elsa

It wasn't a boy. It was a girl. E.S. Elsa Spadaro. I couldn't understand why he hadn't told me. Neither had he told me – although this was understandable – that he was writing a second novel. Too many secrets for my liking.

Chapter Ten

My invasion into Matteo's privacy, carried out with no shame, no trepidation, revealed to me that he probably didn't have one daughter but two. I found loads of photographs, all of two little girls with Matteo, and what's more they looked very like him: big almond eyes, short freckled nose, plump lips and golden curls. Gorgeous.

In these images, Matteo looked the very picture of the happy and responsible father. What motive could he possibly have for hiding this from me?

I spent a while calmly going through the photographs of Matteo and the two little girls, and not knowing what to do or think I looked upwards to the shelves filled with books and spotted an old biscuit tin which I hadn't really noticed before. The thought that people in Sicily also kept photographs in recycled biscuit tins, something I'd always known from my own home, made me smile.

But it wasn't full of photographs. They were letters. A whole pile of letters to Matteo from the two daughters. Some signed by Elsa. Others signed by Ottavia. Some with both names. Elsa and Ottavia Spadaro. Matteo's children.

I snooped through these affectionate, ingenuous letters about new dresses, friends who were cross, and pre-adolescent turmoils. None of the envelopes had the sender's address on the back, just initials on a few. But I found out where they had been sent from because of the postmarks. I didn't look for any special reason, just curiosity. Taormina. Taormina!

I felt a need to share all of these revelations with someone! I thought about calling Sol. But how could I tell my sister that my life, and hers, were being ricocheted into a Matteo Spadaro novel?

I'd call her later, when I'd delved a little further, spoken to Matteo and found out who he really was. I had the strange feeling that until I actually knew the truth about Matteo I couldn't begin to sort out my own truth: what I felt for Matteo and for Raimon, and what I wanted to do with my life. It was difficult to explain, even within myself, but I had the sensation of being turned into a fictional character. Somewhere halfway between the real Blanca and the imaginary Laura. It seemed a little bit as if I could expect Matteo, the creator of Laura, to decide the future of this character – in other words my own future. I wasn't entirely in possession of my own life. Neither did Matteo own his novel, because he had created it – if that's the right word – out of my very reality.

Then, like a flashback in a film, I saw Raimon opposite me the day I demanded an answer from him, when he replied dejectedly 'I haven't lied to you, Blanca, but if you don't believe me, perhaps we've both been deceiving ourselves.'

Weeks had gone by, sleepless nights, painful days, and finally I understood what he meant. I understood and comprehended. It was as if something had removed a large rock from the stone wall which had been erected between us, and through a space of light I saw a little piece of the face of the old Raimon, the one I loved. That sentence, which I had taken as tacit acceptance of his infidelity, now proffered some very different touches: perhaps Raimon was trying to tell me there are many kinds of fidelity and that I was the betrayer, by wrongly robbing him of my confidence.

That night I dreamt I had a daughter and her name was Delight.

The next day, over a cappuccino near the Vucciria, I said to Matteo, rather unwillingly, 'I noticed the other day there was a letter for you from Taormina. Do you know anyone there?' I didn't detect any involuntary muscular movement, not even a blink.

'Yes, of course I do... I know the town very well. I wouldn't have been able to write *Forget the Pain* otherwise, would I?'

It was a good answer; he wasn't saying anything. I didn't want to put him on the ropes too quickly, so we went off to the market to get the things we needed for lunch and went home. The next few days were uneventful, neither glorious nor awful. I was finding myself gradually recovering my strength and energy, at times returning to the Blanca of the old days. However, I still didn't know if I wanted to go home.

I returned, without permission, to Matteo's text:

After she'd told Ivo about the dreadful night of the tragedy, Laura felt closer to him. She also spoke again of the earthquake that her husband's past infidelities had meant to her, and everything she had put into words was no longer festering within her. Laura slowly recuperated her physical and psychological strength. Sicily was putting colour in her cheeks, brightness in her eyes, energy in her smile.

Ivo saw her spring back to life, and he just watched, waiting patiently for her to come into bloom. When the inevitable return to colour and scent arrived, when Laura showed herself to be the woman she was, Ivo would know whether he had fallen in love with her. He was in no hurry. He was all too familiar with the rocky pathways of love and knew not to jump in blindly. After a setback, when least expected, the land can turn fertile in a moment. Laura was brushing the dead leaves away, disentangling her hair, pruning branches, ridding herself of uncertainties. Soon she would emerge, luxuriant, and he would be there, waiting for her.

Ivo had twice before taken the wrong turn; he didn't want any shortcuts, just to get there.

Once I'd read these words, my surprise – absolute amazement in fact – stopped my thought processes dead in their tracks. Ivo, I mean Matteo, was waiting for me to blossom? It would've been better if he'd tried to make it funny. I could almost hear Sol's voice: I bet he's waiting for you to bloom, or for you to wilt.

There was still one drawer of Matteo's desk I hadn't tried. It was locked. Finding the key and opening this drawer suddenly became the main purpose of my life, this fictive and parenthetical life I was living in Sicily.

Chapter Eleven

And so it came to pass that I, Blanca Dausà, girl of integrity and bomb-proof sincerity, began to fake, lie and manipulate without a hint of conscience. What must they have been thinking, men? That they're the only ones who were any good at deception? Raimon's potential betrayal and Matteo's continual untruths were going to be kids' stuff compared to my performance. Matteo Spadaro thought I was 'pruning myself' of afflictions and obsessions in order to offer myself up to him, the writer, like some lovely rose? Well, this fiction was going to receive my collaboration too. I was going to make him think I'd fallen in love; then I'd get to the bottom of his fraud.

The effort required was not beyond me. Matteo was attractive and affectionate, with a great sense of humour and overwhelming warmth. To surrender to his charms – or pretend to – was a simple task. But where the devil did he hide the key to that drawer?

Another week went by with me playing the admirer and also the fount of inspiration. I was living this forced reality and then, as reader, finding it in Matteo's novel. The duplicity was going to end up driving me crazy, not to mention the times I remembered, through the mists, my real life and the mortally threatened marriage I had left behind in Barcelona.

Matteo and I travelled around the south of the island: Ragusa, Modica, Noto, Siracusa. The Castello di Donnafugata, the setting for the great Lampedusa's *The Leopard*. As much as Matteo explained what the name of the castle meant, something like 'Fountain of Health', I couldn't help but think it was an allusion to my personal situation, and that in fact Donnafugata meant 'fugitive woman'.

I was a fugitive from my fears and pain. Since I'd started playing the role of Blanca/Laura, my anxiety attacks had stopped, and now I barely thought about Raimon's unfaithfulness, or debated with myself what the future held for me.

Ivo and Laura, it goes without saying, went to the Donnafugata Castle, as well as all the other beauty spots we'd been to in southern Sicily. They talked about the same things and kissed in virtually the very same places. My words sounded much better, rewritten by Matteo; that's just a fact.

However, the days went by and I couldn't see how I was going to gain access to the locked drawer. Then one morning, just after Matteo had left the house, I had one of my infamous moments of intuition. I'd heard him rummaging around in his study before he went, and I entered the room with my heart beating quickly. I tried the drawer, and... yes, it was unlocked!

Inside was an envelope with a Taormina postmark and handwriting that didn't belong to either of his daughters. On the back, the sender was only 'S'. Clearly Matteo had just read the letter and had put it back in the drawer without locking it. I picked up the envelope, intending to read the contents, but underneath it was a hardcover notebook that caught my attention even more.

I opened it and immediately saw what it was. It was a private diary. Every page was handwritten, and in a clear and rounded hand, and the date every so often.

Matteo writing a diary? No, this wasn't his doctor's handwriting.

I chose a page at random and started to read:

Monday, 12th March. I cannot concentrate on anything. I wake up and my first thought is about him, or her, or the two of them. The day becomes a continual, and often failed, attempt to direct my mind to other issues. I've learned that for me it's easier to latch on to little everyday things than to the ones which really matter. So when I feel threatened by this obsession I make mental notes of the shopping list: I'm out of coffee and I must buy some kiwis. I'm not sure if I'm not going mad.

These words weren't new to me. I'd read them before. How come? Who'd written all this?

Friday, 24th April. My life seems to me like a sequence of errors and wrong moves. I've been wrong in all the most important things in life: my selection of the person to share it with, choosing a career which has become dull, having two daughters whose upbringing in a happy environment I just can't envisage.

Whoever the woman who'd written this diary was, she was having a really bad time of it.... Woman who'd written...? Why woman? I went back over the page I'd just read. There was nowhere I could logically deduce it was a woman. So why had I just assumed it? From the handwriting? From what it said? Or because I'd somehow felt, or simply *knew*, it was a woman?

I went to the last page.

Saturday, 6th June. I am alone, looking out at the sea, not knowing where to start rebuilding my shattered life. What do I look for to prop me up and how do I go about making sure I don't fail again?

I feel alone, envious, yearning, furious, sad. It's been hard to admit, as the years have gone by, that happiness consists of the absence of pain. I have gradually come to accept it as the price you pay to be an adult. Does this mean that from now on my only aim in life must be reduced to minimising pain? Doing that, forgetting the pain, will definitely be the only way to survive.

'Forget the pain to survive.' Bruna. *Forget the Pain*. Of course! I felt my heart was going to burst on me, it was racing so fast! So Matteo had written an early draft of the novel as a first-person diary? But this wasn't his handwriting.... Whose was it? Was there a Bruna whose diary Matteo had stolen? Was that what it was? Was *Forget the Pain* the life of someone, like his new novel was my life?

I made myself a coffee and lit a cigarette (I must give up), and as I watched the smoke curling upwards, a tiny but dazzling light came on in my head. That B on the back of the envelope with the Taormina postmark.... The pieces of the jigsaw began to fit very easily. I opened the drawer and took out the envelope. There were only three or four lines of cold, opaque computer print. First shot off-target: I'd thought the writing in the letter would match the diary's. The text was also very sterile: *Mr Merisi will contact you to detail the alterations to the monthly expenses, but he has asked me to put this down in writing. Please reply without delay.*

It wasn't signed with an initial on its own, but with the whole name. And the name was the last piece in the puzzle: Bruna.

Bruna. *My* Bruna. The Bruna in the book. Massimo's Bruna. Matteo's Bruna.

All I could do that afternoon was build up my rage into a ball to spit out at Matteo when I saw him come through the door.

When he put the key in the lock, I was waiting on the sofa with letters arranged around me, photographs of the girls, Bruna's diary, and pages of the second novel I'd printed off. Exposing, obscenely, his privacy; shamelessly laying bare his misery.

He collapsed in a heap next to me, as if every drop of strength had deserted him. I thought he was drowning. But he took in air and released it with the effort you use to achieve the calm required to avoid violence. When he looked at me, it was indeed violence that I saw in his eyes.

'What the fuck were you thinking?'

Sicilians are the best out of all the Italians at swearing and I readied myself for a profusion of foul language. I wasn't scared; I was sure that whatever he said would flow past me harmlessly.

Matteo began to gather up papers and photos energetically, almost agressively, mumbling through his teeth a hundred curses which I couldn't hear, but sensed. When he'd put everything in a pile on the table, he came up to me, inches from my face. His eyes were in flames.

'What sort of person are you? I invite you into my house, and my time, and because you work your way into my bed you think you can work your way into my computer as well, into my life?'

Although my voice was a little creaky, I was able to respond: 'I didn't work my way into your bed.'

Matteo interrupted me, violently. 'Yes you did! You turned up here all the victim, displaying your wounds all over the place, and you were very grateful for the comforting I gave you. You don't even know for sure if your man has done the dirty on you or if you've made the whole thing up! I thought you needed some affection and all you wanted to do was to go through my desk! Get the fuck out of my house!'

I felt my chin trembling and swore to myself that I wouldn't cry in front of Matteo. I knew there was an element of truth in what he said, but I wasn't going to be intimidated by his tone of voice or his Italian cinema histrionics. With all the dignity I could find in me, I lifted my eyes and looked straight at him.

'You're not a writer. You're a liar. You steal other people's stories. And you're a cynical man.'

He was silent for a few moments, as if he wasn't sure, and then said:

'I did not steal Bruna's diary; she gave it to me so I could see at first hand the pain she went through. It was her way to get revenge. And I don't need to give you any more explanations.'

In the moments that followed, I heard all the sounds that filled the silence in the house: the motor in the fridge, the water running through the pipes, and the clock on the wall. I thought about how I had been affected by reading *Forget the*

Pain and I understood why I had been. The pain was real, and I had adopted it. I then realised I had to pull myself together to feel that pain again, and even so I didn't think I'd be able to entirely. Maybe I'd released myself from it. Maybe my pain wasn't real.

I said, very softly, 'You could have changed her name.'

Matteo looked at me, with what seemed to be a smile in his eyes.

'Bruna's? There's no other name for her.'

I collected myself, holding his gaze as long as I could, because I finally understood, a little.

He loved her! Matteo still loved this woman! It was the best revenge possible. I even abandoned the thought of talking to him about the novel he was writing about me and all my secrecies. Matteo and his novels meant nothing to me any more.

It took me just ten minutes to stuff my clothes into my bag. I collected things from the bathroom. I got to the front door without a word from Matteo, who was still in the sitting room. I stopped for a second, bag in one hand, about to open the door with the other. Was I leaving without a tearful goodbye? Yes. And with a good slam of the door too. What a relief to get away from a man as easily as that! Goodbye Massimo/Matteo!

I walked through the streets of the centre of Palermo with a calmness which was outrageous given what I was going through. I felt proud I'd revealed Matteo Spadaro for what he was before I got hurt, and feeling no longer totally exposed and vulnerable was a comfort to me.

Back in the little hotel in the Piazza Marina, I wrote down every detail of what had happened. When I got home, I'd tell Sol the whole story and she'd be speechless.

Then I spent a couple of hours stretched out on the bed,

hands behind my head, looking up at the blue ceiling of the Sicilian hotel. I saw the shapes of different faces changing from one to another. A Matteo with a handsome smile, a Bruna I hadn't met but imagined. A papier maché Massimo, like a Venetian mask. A circumspect Raimon, but with a puerile context in his eyes. 'Maybe you made the whole thing up'; that sentence of Matteo's began to write itself in neon lights. What if Raimon had been telling the truth? If he hadn't been unfaithful? The idea was hurting my head so much that I brushed it aside.

So Bruna, 'my' Bruna from *Forget the Pain*, really existed? The woman I had felt so close to, with whom I'd identified to such excess, she was a real woman who lived in Taormina with her daughters, Matteo's daughters.

Could I leave Sicily without trying to find her? No way. I wanted to see her, to discover if she was like I had pictured her, if she was anything like the image I'd created of her, over time, in my brain.

I wanted to talk to her, tell her who I was and why I felt such closeness although we didn't know each other in the slightest. I wanted to ask her what her life was like and how things had been after the break-up and if she was happy without Matteo.

Once I'd decided on this I fell asleep. I woke eight hours later, rested and optimistic. The day was bright and the sky over Sicily blue and hopeful.

I phoned Sol to tell her I was okay and was going to stay another week in Sicily and then come home. She said that sounded all right: you'd better not wait any longer to talk to Raimon. I thought of him on the edge, about to lose it, and sent him a text which I hoped was reassuring but measured.

The thought that he wouldn't want to listen to me when I got home was beginning to concern me.

After a while I received a laconic reply of 'OK' which made me well up, and very soon afterwards an 'I love you', which felt like a thick woolly jumper when you're freezing.

By noon I'd rented a car to get to Taormina. For the first time since I'd left Barcelona, I was on a journey where the destination was more important than what I'd left behind.

I drove down the motorway which follows the coastline of north-eastern Sicily and before Capo d'Orlando I saw the sign for the turning to Taormina. The road to take me to the town of *Forget the Pain* was lined with orange and lemon trees. Sweet oranges and bitter lemons. What awaited me in Taormina?

Chapter Twelve

In Taormina, the air smelled of orange. I immediately thought of my mother, who'd have said 'It smells clean'. And that's how it was, the smell of baby lotion, lavender, cleanliness.

I checked into a small hotel which was both luxurious and expensive. In the week at most I planned to stay in the town, I'd run through the last bit of my savings, which had started to dissolve the moment I left Barcelona.

I walked down the Corso Umberto, stopping at the windows of the patisserie with the look of a salivating child, determined to give myself, for those few days, every innocent pleasure imaginable.

To get started on this mission as soon as possible, I sat down on the terrace of the Wünderbar café, knowing full well that a cappuccino was going to cost me an arm and a leg. What did that matter, when you think of all the tourists who do the same, in the same place as Liz Taylor once did?

As I enjoyed the cappuccino, for which they did indeed charge an exhorbitant price, a young woman with two young girls passed by. My heart jumped and took a moment to recover itself. Bruna? Bruna and her daughters?

Lighting a cigarette (I really must give up) helped me get back to my senses. It was just too improbable, not to say impossible, that after half an hour in Taormina, and in one of the busiest and most central streets of the town, I was going to come across the person I was looking for, like someone who sticks their hand into the haystack and finds the needle first time.

The Sicilian with the two children stopped by a shop window, quite near me; a man, who could've been her father, called out 'Benedetta!' Although I'd been staring at the back of her head for quite some time, I managed to pull myself away.

I looked at the scrap of paper where I'd written down Bruna's address. Only one of the letters from his daughters Matteo had kept included the full address: Ottavia Spadaro, Via Rizzo 31, Taormina.

At the hotel, they provided me with a detailed steet plan of the town. It was simple enough to locate Via Rizzo. It wasn't far from where I was and, although I was very tired, I couldn't wait until the next day.

I walked through the streets of Taormina with the map in my hand, observing everything closely and stopping opposite houses which drew my attention. Unhurried.

It was around eight in the evening when I reached Via Rizzo. It was pointless to expect that Bruna, with two small children, might be about to arrive home at that time of night, but I wanted to see her house. The house where Matteo and Bruna had lived for so many years, the house where the deceit had been shaped, the house which Matteo/Massimo had abandoned for a fleeting romance.

But number 31 wasn't a house, as I'd always imagined; it was a five-storey building with large balconies overlooking the street. I stood on the pavement opposite and looked up. Each flat had two balconies – two flats on each floor, I worked out. I had no idea which was Bruna's.

There were lights burning in most of the windows. All these Sicilian families having their dinner, or laying the table as they listened to the day's news. Behind the extreme right-hand balcony on the third floor I saw little shadows moving... Elsa and Ottavia, Matteo's children.... Or maybe not. Maybe they weren't even at home that evening. Or maybe the girls were already in bed and Bruna was sitting behind any one of the building's other windows, enjoying a moment's peace at the end of the day.

There was no way that this woman, alone and devastated – or happy, who knows? – could imagine I would be there across the road, feeling her presence. That I was watching out for her, knowing her life, her pain, her lost love. That I shared with her the experience of deceit and had tasted the kisses of betraying lips, and had also become a character in a Spadaro novel. So many things in common and she had no idea I even existed.

The next morning I'd go and search for her and find out if she looked sad or radiant, if there was forgiveness or rancour in her eyes, if there were any tiny cracks where love was emerging.

At that very moment, someone opened the third-floor balcony window and a dark figure was outlined in the dim light of the street lamp. The face wasn't visible, but it was a woman, or possibly a girl. A delicate body which could equally be that of an adolescent or the mother of a family. Straight hair fluttered in the evening breeze. She leant on the balcony railing to look down onto the street. She must have seen me standing motionless on the other side of the road, but I couldn't make out her eyes enough to know if she was looking at me or not. Was this Bruna, who'd sensed my presence? Or was it just some Sicilian woman who'd wanted to see if the night had cooled down? The shadow disappeared from the balcony and I went back to my hotel room. The next day, when I met Bruna, I was going to ask her whether she'd been out on her balcony the night before.

First thing in the morning I was in Via Rizzo and I didn't have to wait long. A little before eight the door to number 31 opened and I heard the flapping of children's voices. I recognised Matteo's daughters, the girls in the photograph, Elsa and Ottavia. With them was their mother, Bruna. My Bruna.

She was slim, not very tall and with straight dark hair down to her shoulders. She was casually dressed, in jeans and a sky-blue T-shirt. She had a shoulder bag and was carrying a file. She could easily have passed for a student. She walked right in front of me, not looking at me, hurrying up the children who were playing with whatever.

'*Andiamo! Sono le otto passate!*'

Her accent was even more delightful than Matteo's.

I followed them unobtrusively, a few yards behind, to the school. The two girls were all laughter, and said goodbye to their mother very affectionately. She, Bruna, was smiling all the while. As they went into the school she looked towards where I was standing and for an instant our eyes met. It seemed to me that hers weren't smiling as much as her lips.

I pictured her entering the classroom, greeting her pupils with a bright '*Buon giorno!*' The school seemed welcoming, not very big.

I thought everything about Taormina was just the right size. Small enough not be oppressive, busy enough not be boring.

Before I'd left the hotel that morning I'd seen on the wall a piece of Maupassant that someone had framed. 'To anyone who has only one day to see Sicily and asks me "Where do I go?" I reply Taormina, without hesitation. It is but a setting; however, it is a setting which sums up everything on earth that can draw the eye, the imagination, and the spirit.'

I had the entire day to check out the truth of Maupassant's words. Until mid-afternoon when I'd go to the school, find Bruna as she was leaving and introduce myself.

Map in hand, I went off to Piazza Vittorio Emanuele to see the Palazzo Corvaja. It was recommended in all the guidebooks, but I had a very special interest: this was a scene I already knew through literature. It was when she was taking that group of schoolchildren to the Palazzo Corvaja that she saw, from a distance, Matteo with Isabella for the first time. They were in Piazza Vittorio Emanuele.

I retraced her steps and it was easy to imagine what Bruna felt on seeing them. There, in the middle of the square, I pictured Raimon with the woman I'd imagined but didn't know and a shudder went down my spine like a bolt of lightning.

I saw Taormina's renowned Greek Theatre and went through the ritual of sitting down facing the stage to look over to the silhouette of Mount Etna and the houses of Giardini-Naxos.

Finally I went to the Villa Comunale gardens, where Bruna had vomited out her anguish way back then. As she had done, I marvelled at the park full of fruit trees and myriad-coloured flowers whose names I didn't know. And the volcano imposing its mighty presence.

Time was getting on and soon it would be four in the afternoon. When the school gates opened and the shriek of children's voices erupted, I was in the square opposite, sitting on a doorstep because my legs had given up on me. I was dying of anxiety and emotion. I was about to meet Bruna. The real Bruna, whose story had changed my life. I didn't exactly know what I needed to say to initiate such an unusual conversation and above all I didn't know how she'd react to my confessions. 'Hello, good afternoon, my name's Blanca and I've come here to Sicily from Barcelona after I read your ex-husband's novel, which is the story of your life.' Should I confess to her that I'd met Matteo and had lived with him in Palermo? I didn't know what I ought to say to her; I just knew I wanted to tell her that I felt she was very close to me.

She came out with another teacher, chatting away animatedly, and stopped before crossing the road. She was waiting for the children. First to emerge was Ottavia with her pigtail half-unravelled, and then Elsa, who was in much less of a state. Both of them hugged their mother and kissed her on the cheeks amid laughter and she was laughing herself. Looking at Bruna there was no indication of sadness. She was a young mother, healthy and happy, meeting up with her daughters at the end of the school day, two playful little girls asking her when they'd be having tea. Not a shred of tragedy in that scene. Absolute normality, everyday happiness.

She crossed the road with one daughter either side of her, arms over their shoulders, and as I watched her go past I turned into a statue. Then, like a robot, I followed them when they went into a little coffee shop on the square and sat at the next table, feeling like a spy and an idiot.

I could hear their conversation perfectly, although because

the children were talking at breakneck speed, and frequently both at the same time, I missed a lot of the words.

Elsa was saying that her class was putting on a play, and she'd been chosen for one of the main parts. Ottavia told her mother that the basketball coach had chosen her in the starting line-up for that afternoon's game. Elsa was complaining about the geography teacher, who had a thing about her and never gave her more than six out of ten. Ottavia reminded her mother that she'd promised to get her some new trainers.

Bruna was nodding, shaking her head, laughing or scowling as required, and occasionally trying to keep their voices down with hand gestures.

I sipped on a beer as I watched. The girls looked like their mother but had Matteo's eyes. All of a sudden I felt a compassion for Matteo that I'd never have imagined. I thought of him alone in that untidy house in Palermo, missing out on the daily stories these girls told, their bright smiles and their unruly hugs.

Matteo alone. Bruna without Matteo. Isabella alone. Elsa and Ottavia without their father. The only good thing which had come out of all of this was a novel.

But no novel is worth so many tears.

I lit a cigarette and took a gulp of my beer.

'*Scusi*, have you got a light?'

Bruna had just spoken to me. In the musical accent and low-pitched voice which I'd been listening to secretly for a while. I looked at her and she smiled at me with a face full of brightness.

I passsed her my lighter, returning her smile, but I was unable to articulate a single word. It was a see-through lighter with a turquoise blue liquid inside and little starfish floating around.

Matteo had bought it for me in a souvenir shop in Stromboli.

Little Ottavia let out a shriek: '*Che carino! Mi piace!*' Her mother lit her cigarette and put the lighter back down on my table. '*Grazie mille*'.

I looked at the girl, I looked at Bruna, and I remembered Matteo offering me the lighter. I said to her, 'Keep it, it's a present.'

Bruna protested, but Ottavia looked at me gratefully and her mother conceded.

'That's very kind of you, thank you.'

'Not at all.'

Bruna and the girls went back into the depths of their chaotic family conversation and I remained silent, knowing I'd missed my opportunity.

But there was nothing I could say to her. This Bruna wasn't my Bruna. She wasn't a character in a fictional tale, she was a mother having tea with her daughters after school and couldn't have been more real. This Bruna wasn't the face of pain; she was a young, healthy woman who seemed content, and had, possibly, a hint of sadness in her eyes.

Who hasn't?

Maybe I was less real than she. This Blanca, sitting in a coffee shop in Taormina, miles away from the people I love, having left behind a kleptomaniac writer who'd turned me into a character.

As I pondered, Bruna and the children had got up and gone to the counter to pay for their tea. As they passed by me, Bruna offered me her hand.

'Here, I wouldn't want you to be without a light.'

She gave me a white lighter with red lettering. 'I love Taormina'. By the time I turned to thank her, she'd already left.

Chapter Thirteen

As the plane took off, the butterflies in my stomach were still, wings quiet. I didn't want to look at Sicily through the tiny window, but its image filled my thoughts, in Cinemascope and Technicolor.

The parentheses had closed. The days of fictional holidays were over, the love affairs out of the movies, the characters in novels, the dreams of Goethe and the music of Bellini. Palermo, Taormina and Catania went back to being their busy selves, Etna puffed and blowed, Bruna got back to the routine of her teaching, and I reacquainted myself with the real Blanca. I was going home a little bit more experienced, a little less naïve, and much freer. Older and wiser.

Sol was there at the airport waiting for me, with her protective and vital hug. Her unquestioning interest. Her rock-solid confidence.

The hugs we all hope to find when we return from a

dangerous journey safe and sound by the skin of our teeth.

The conversation with Raimon was relaxed, easy, full of turns and pauses. Both of us tried hard to find a delicate balance between penance and pardon, shame and pride, dignity and love.

Words entwined and were left cleanly placed on the table, tidy and light. Then caresses performed the role of a gust of air and the promises and repentance floated away and all that was left was tenderness.

Forget the pain in order to survive, Bruna's recipe, resounded in my brain. To live more love, more future, more pain, more life.

'Do you love me?' asked Raimon.

'Yes,' I said.

'Forever?'

'Probably.'

* * *

The Cat was translated into Catalan at the end of the year. By then, in Italy, half a million people had read it and the name of its author, Matteo Spadaro, had been inscribed in the pantheon of Europe's best-selling novelists.

Blanca didn't do the translation. She couldn't even be bothered to read it. She knew what happened.

The new year began with bright days and unusually spring-like temperatures. At the beginning of February, the publishers asked her to do a rather dull book about European Union commerce. Her depleted financial situation meant she had to accept every translation she was offered and work all hours, concentrating through the boredom of it. She opened up dictionaries as if solving algebraic calculations. Looking for synonyms for words like tariffs, duties, taxes, liens didn't arouse her emotions, and that was exactly what she needed in her state of mind.

Then one February morning she looked out of the window of her little workroom. She didn't do it deliberately, just a momentary lapse of concentration. Her eyes wandered away and through the glass she saw the slightest of clouds which looked like an island in the middle of the blue.

The rooftops and aerials were a jumble and then she noticed, right in front of her, a patch of white. Next door's almond tree had come into blossom. For a moment she thought that everything she held in her memory had flown out of the window, as if she'd blown on those little round flowers, dandelions, the 'little angels', and the white powdery dust had settled on the branches of the tree.

She typed the last full stop on the EU commerce translation. Then she opened a new document. One last look out at the white of the almond tree and she wrote two words, slowly, with a pleasure she hadn't known before.

Dear Bruna,

A Note by the Author

When I write I always have the feeling I have done in some way a Matteo Spadaro, that somehow I have purloined stories and feelings from people I know. I often ask their permission, so I feel more relaxed about it. Still, I want to state here my special thanks to two people.

Two women who have gifted me wise words, in both cases the result of pain endured. Thank you Joana, and thank you Maria Rosa.

Translated Fiction

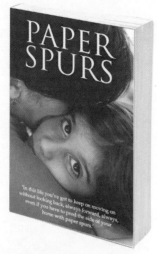

parthianbooks.com